Annie Fought The Desire
To Fling Caution To The Wind

and accept Sam's invitation. She was still in love with him, but another night in his bed could only expose her to more hurt in the end. In the clear light of day she was forced to acknowledge that Sam still didn't need her, or anyone—not really, not at the deep, meaningful level where she needed him.

"Not a good idea," she said finally.

"I think it's a terrific idea," he said quietly.

Annie thought of his spotless house. She tried to remember if she'd left her towel on the bathroom floor after her shower that morning. She feared she had. She'd probably left the cap off the toothpaste, as well. Annie sighed inwardly, telling herself that she and Sam probably didn't have a chance of making it together, even if he did love her.

They were destined to drive each other crazy—in more ways than one.

Dear Reader:

I hope you've been enjoying 1989, our "Year of the Man" at Silhouette Desire. Every one of the twelve authors who are contributing a *Man of the Month* has created a very special someone for your reading pleasure. Each man is unique, and each author's style and characterization give you a different insight into her man's story.

From January to December, 1989 will be a twelve-month extravaganza spotlighting one book each month with special cover treatment as a tribute to the Silhouette Desire hero—our *Man of the Month*!

Created by your favorite authors, these men are utterly captivating—and I think Mr. June, Annette Broadrick's Quinn McNamara, will be simply... *Irresistible*! One of Lass Small's Lambert sisters gets a very special man in July. *Man of the Month* Graham Rawlins may start as the *Odd Man Out*, but that doesn't last long....

Yours,

Isabel Swift

Senior Editor & Editorial Coordinator

JEANNE STEPHENS
Sharing California

Silhouette Desire

Published by Silhouette Books New York

America's Publisher of Contemporary Romance

SILHOUETTE BOOKS
300 East 42nd St., New York, N.Y. 10017

ISBN: 0-373-05504-8

First Silhouette Books printing June 1989

Printed in the U.S.A.

JEANNE STEPHENS

loves to travel, but she's always glad to get home to Oklahoma. This incurable romantic and mother of three loves reading ("I'll read anything!" she says), needlework, photography, long walks—during which she works out her latest books—and, of course, her own romantic hero: her husband.

One

Annie heard the telephone ringing before she reached her front door. She anchored the stack of file folders with her chin and ran. Her high heels clicked against the paved walk like loud firecrackers exploding in the evening quiet.

This section of the apartment complex was open to adults only. No children or pets allowed. Except for the occasional late-night party, Annie never heard her neighbors, and because of the long hours she spent at the office, she rarely saw them.

At her door she fumbled blindly for her keys while keeping her chin on the stack of folders. "Oh, damn," she muttered as she riffled through the contents of her bag, identifying each item by feel. The keys weren't there.

Had she left them in the car? Wait.... She plunged her hand into the pocket of her suit jacket and found the keys. She couldn't remember dropping them there when she got out of the car, but then she barely recalled driving home. She was so tired, she was punchy.

The phone was still ringing as she shoved open the door and stumbled into a chair. The caller was persistent, if nothing else. Probably somebody selling light bulbs, Annie thought irritably.

She had almost succeeded in regaining her balance after colliding with the chair when the precarious stack of folders slid out of her arms. The contents scattered over the chair and brown shag carpet.

"Double damn." Annie groaned and lunged for the phone. "Yes?" She paused to catch her breath. Static crackled in her ear. "Hello?"

"Miss Ann Marie Malloy, please." The female voice sounded far away, as though it echoed from the far end of a tunnel.

Annie dropped to the couch and kicked off her shoes. "Speaking."

"Please hold for...—wood." Most of the name was lost in static.

"I'm sorry," Annie said. "Who did you say is calling?" She received no response, though. The woman had put her on hold. Between bursts of static, Annie heard music playing. She was tempted to hang up. She hadn't nearly killed herself getting to the phone to listen to elevator music. On second thought, the poor connection probably meant the call was long distance. It could be important. Maybe it was her parents, who'd been traveling in their RV for three weeks. They were due home today, but they might have been delayed. Annie waited, praying that if it was her parents, their news wasn't bad. She combed her fingers through her brown curls and pinched the bridge of her nose to ease the headache building behind her eyes.

A male voice boomed in her ear. "Miss Malloy?"

Annie's frayed nerves jangled. "Yes. Who is this, please?"

"Jason Smallwood calling from L.A., Miss Malloy.... I've been trying...for some time." Again some of the caller's words were drowned out, but Annie surmised he was saying he'd been trying to reach her.

"Have we met, Mr. Smallwood?"

"No. I'm with Benton...and Smallwood, Attorneys-at-Law. Are you related to Gerald Frederick Malloy?"

"Freddy? Yes, we're first cousins. What has Freddy got to do with—"

The attorney cut her off. "Apparently you haven't heard. Mr. Malloy was killed...wreck on one of our freeways ten days ago.... Died instantly...funeral last week...unable to reach you. We had an old address and phone number. We couldn't reach your parents at their Florida address, either."

"I moved recently, and my folks have been on vacation."

It was another moment before the full meaning of his garbled words sank in. When it did, Annie's tired eyes stung with hot tears. She squeezed the lids shut. "Oh no."

She hadn't heard from Freddy in more than a year. At that time he'd been out of work. Having lost yet another job, he'd moved in with Annie, and she'd been going through a difficult period emotionally herself. After coming home from work to find Freddy still in his pajamas for about the tenth time, she'd lost her temper and accused him of not even trying to find another job. The next morning Freddy was gone. He'd moved out in the middle of the night, leaving only a note thanking her for her hospitality and promising to repay her "when his ship came in." She'd had no word from him since. Poor Freddy.

"...my sympathy...executor of Mr. Malloy's estate..." Smallwood was saying.

Annie dashed a tear from her cheek and strained to hear. "Freddy's estate?" As far as Annie knew, Freddy had never owned anything but a few clothes and a broken-down car. Did you need an executor for that?

"The other heir can be in my office Saturday the fifteenth for the reading of the will...you be there?"

"Saturday, April fifteen?" Only four days away. "I don't know." She didn't want to go all the way to California to learn she'd inherited a car with four flat tires and a leaky radiator. And who was the other heir? Freddy's only living relatives were Annie and her parents.

"Is it really necessary for me to come out there?"

There was a burst of static on the line and then Smallwood's voice boomed, "...imperative!...reserved a room at the Sheraton for Friday night...pick up your ticket at the American desk...take possession...your inheritance...California...."

"I can't hear you. Maybe you should hang up and call me back. This line is terrible."

Smallwood must not have understood her, or he simply chose to ignore the suggestion. "...pencil and paper?" he was saying.

Annie grabbed a notepad and pen. "Yes. Go on."

He gave her the address of the hotel and of his office, where the reading of the will would take place Saturday morning at ten. Then his voice faded away and static stuttered on the line.

"Hello? Are you still there?" Annie stabbed the disconnect button a few times. "Mr. Smallwood?"

The operator came on the line. "Your party has hung up, ma'am."

"Great." Annie dropped the receiver into the cradle and leaned her head back against the couch. Freddy was dead. It didn't seem possible. "I didn't really mean to kick you out, Freddy," she sighed. "I was in a bad mood and I took it out on you. I always wanted to apologize and now it's too late."

She found a crumpled tissue in her jacket pocket and dabbed at her eyes. She should have tried harder to learn where Freddy went when he'd moved out. Maybe he'd finally stayed with a job for more than a few weeks, Annie thought hopefully, wanting to believe that Freddy had known success in some area during his last year of life.

It had to have been a job that didn't require his taking orders, though. Freddy had always hated taking orders. This had made him a difficult teenager and contributed to his losing one job after another. Every time he did find employment, instead of concentrating on the work assigned to him, he'd spent his time conjuring up get-rich-quick schemes, none of which ever panned out.

In spite of knowing that Freddy brought most of his problems on himself, Annie had always had a soft spot for him. Which was why she'd let him move in with her whenever he was unemployed. After all, Freddy had played a crucial role in her life; he'd introduced her to Sam Bennington, his childhood chum.

Thinking of Sam—even seeing his name in the Oklahoma City newspaper—always caused a lump to lodge in Annie's throat. That she still had that reaction, after more than a year, filled her with self-disgust. For heaven's sake, she had been the one who'd wanted to split up.... Well, perhaps "wanted" wasn't the right word.

Annie sat up and switched on a table lamp. Enough, she told herself. Thinking of Sam was counterproductive—it depressed her. She didn't need that on top of everything else. She took off her jacket and phoned her parents in Florida. They were full of the sights they'd seen on their vacation, and she had to break in on her mother to tell them the news.

After hanging up, she knelt on the carpet and began stuffing the strewn papers back into their proper folders. As an accounts manager in the real estate department of an Oklahoma City savings and loan, she interviewed applicants for home mortgage loans, checked their references and guided those who were approved by the loan committee through the required paperwork. She was also responsible for keeping track of their accounts, seeing that they made their mortgage payments on time and contacting them when a payment was late.

Due to the recent downturn in Oklahoma's economy, more and more of Annie's accounts had become delinquent, forcing her to spend much of her time performing the duties of a one-person collection agency. Since she could reach most of these people at home only in the evening, she frequently worked late and sometimes brought the remiss accounts home with her.

Her job had been a lifesaver when she broke up with Sam, and she'd buried herself in it. Lately, though, the work was putting her under a great deal of stress. She disliked dunning people for money. Worse, she listened to their hard-luck stories and sympathized with *them* instead of the savings and loan.

Three times she'd gone to Harry Layman, her boss, with the intention of resigning. But Harry always succeeded in talking her out of it, verbally painting a picture of the fantastic future she'd have with the savings and loan if she would only be patient a little while longer. Harry usually ended these mini pep talks with, "The economy will bounce back—it always has before. The sky's the limit, Annie. Trust me." Annie felt like a rabbit with a juicy carrot dangling in front of her, always just out of reach.

After she'd sorted the papers, Annie stacked the files on her desk beside the telephone. But she needed some aspirin, a shower and nourishment before she could face making any collection calls.

Half an hour later, wearing a pink cotton nightgown and robe, Annie stuck a frozen dinner in the microwave and poured a glass of milk. She ate at the table in the kitchen alcove overlooking the apartment's swimming pool. It was mid-April and the pool hadn't yet been uncovered and cleaned for the summer season; the patio area surrounding it was deserted. It was a tranquil scene, and Annie preferred it that way.

Her thoughts returned to the call from the Los Angeles attorney. She'd gleaned the essential information, but she wished they'd had a better connection. Freddy had named her in his will, left her a bequest—but what? Smallwood had said something that sounded like "California."

Annie replayed the conversation again. She was still certain he'd said "California," but that made no sense. Obviously she hadn't heard what came after "California." California real estate? Or maybe Freddy had started a business, using California as part of the company name. But that didn't sound like Freddy. He hadn't had the drive to stay with a business enterprise long enough to get it off the ground.

Could it be that one of Freddy's get-rich-schemes had paid off, after all? Annie let herself fantasize about what she'd do if she suddenly came into a vast amount of money, but only for a few minutes. It made her feel guilty to think of profiting from Freddy's death. Besides, it was too incredible. Whatever she had inherited from Freddy, it wasn't likely to have much monetary value. Probably some fake antiques or worthless uranium stock. Regardless, it was sweet of Freddy to have remembered her in his will. Evidently he hadn't held her harsh words, the last he'd heard her utter, against her.

The only thing she could do for Freddy now was to be there for the reading of the will, even if it did seem like an unnecessary gesture—a case of too little, too late. Surely whatever legalities were involved could be handled by mail. But Smallwood had taken care of her plane fare and hotel room. She could fly to L.A. Friday afternoon and return Saturday evening. The change of scenery might be good for her.

Annie stepped from a cab in front of a tall, white stone office building. A discreet brass plaque beside the revolving door read Benton, Frick, Heldenberger, and Smallwood, Attorneys-at-Law.

She pushed open the door and entered a large, maroon-carpeted foyer. The receptionist sitting at the teakwood desk smiled and said, "You must be Miss Malloy."

"Yes." Unless business offices in L.A. stayed open on Saturday, which Annie doubted, the receptionist was getting paid overtime simply to greet her and direct her to the meeting place. She looked around the plush foyer. Clearly, Benton, Frick, Heldenberger, and Smallwood were doing all right.

"Mr. Smallwood's office is 105 at the end of the hall. Would you like me to show you?"

"No, thanks. I can find it." Annie smoothed the silk skirt of her teal blue shirtwaist and caught a glimpse of herself in a gilt-framed mirror as she walked down the hall, her footsteps muffled by the thick carpet. She paused in front of the door marked 105 long enough to run a comb through her short, dark curls. Then she opened her compact and freshened her lip gloss.

The flight from Oklahoma City the previous day had included a change of planes in Denver. There, the plane with all its passengers had sat on the runway for three hours waiting for takeoff clearance from the control tower. She had arrived at the L.A. hotel late, tired and disheveled. Consequently she'd overslept this morning and had barely had time to dress and apply a few dashes of makeup before phoning for a cab.

She dropped the compact and lip gloss into her bag and opened the door. There was no one in Smallwood's private reception area but a tall man in a navy jacket and gray trousers standing at one of the long windows, his back to the door.

Annie froze in her tracks.

Sam Bennington. She recognized the casually styled sandy hair and the set of the broad shoulders instantly. Reflexively her hands clenched and she swallowed to force down the lump in her throat. *Ridiculous*, she told herself as she fought the tension that gripped her. Once, a long time ago, she and Sam had been lovers, and now they weren't. That's all there was to it; one mistake shouldn't be allowed to affect her for the rest of her life.

A faint, pleasantly masculine odor drifted toward Annie. She recognized it as the after-shave Sam had worn when they were together. It annoyed her that the familiar aroma brought with it a flood of memories.

During the fifteen months since their breakup, she had avoided places where she might run into Sam. If she came upon his name in a newspaper article about a bar association function or a court case in which he represented one of the litigants, she would immediately turn the page. Sam didn't need her; he didn't need anyone. He was out of her life, by her own decision. She was confident that when she did chance to meet Sam again, nothing would be left of what had been between them.

Now, after a single whiff of his after-shave, she was no longer so sure.

He must have sensed her presence then, for he turned. She saw that physically he was the same. His face was narrow, its strong bones at variance with an oddly tender mouth. At least it was tender until he set his jaw and the lips thinned, as they did now. His sandy hair was as she remembered it, a bit too long, grazing his ears and back collar. His smoke-gray eyes held the same guarded expression that had finally defeated her.

"Hello, Annie." His voice held no emotion.

Annie's mouth went dry and her palms began to sweat. He was so still, like a hunter waiting for his prey to come within rifle range. His expression didn't change, while Annie's thoughts whirled with emotions and remembered sensations.

"Sam, what—" She had been about to ask what he was doing there, but all at once she remembered her telephone conversation with Smallwood. Hadn't he mentioned another heir? Obviously, Freddy had named Sam in his will, too. It was the only thing that made any sense.

"You're the other heir," Sam echoed her thoughts. "I wasn't informed."

What did he mean by that? Would he have refused to come if he'd known he'd see her? And must he take that offended air with her? Annie wondered furiously, as though he'd been tricked into being in the same room with her.

"Neither was I." She managed to make eye contact with him with outward calm, but her stomach muscles tightened.

He gave her a long, quizzical look. "Must be Freddy's idea of a joke."

"Freddy always did have a perverse sense of humor," she countered. But she didn't think Freddy had meant it as a joke. She remembered those weeks, the last time Freddy camped out in her apartment. He'd moved in soon after she broke up with Sam, and up until the night he left, he'd never stopped urging her to relent, to call Sam and apologize, to go back to him. Freddy seemed to feel he had a personal stake in their relationship because they were the two people closest to him.

Annie had a growing conviction that this was Freddy's last-ditch effort to get her and Sam back together. With his customary disregard for the facts, Freddy had believed in the impossible to the end.

Sam stuffed one hand in his trouser pocket and spread the other on the back of a leather chair. Annie stood straight and tense, rooted to a spot just inside the door. With those guarded gray eyes, he seemed to be studying her. Even in his relaxed posture there was a sense of hardness, of self-containment and total self-reliance. Annie hated him for it.

Her brown eyes glinted with an emotion he couldn't decipher. Though she met his gaze calmly, he sensed volatility just beneath the surface. Annie was emotional by nature, passionate about causes and people that meant something to her. It was one of the things he had admired in her, that had drawn him to her against his better judgment.

"You haven't changed at all, Annie."

"Neither have you. I don't suppose people do, really." Why was her throat threatening to close and cut off her breath?

"Change is too painful for most people." He tugged at his tie.

It was the first gesture of unease she'd seen him make. Perhaps he wasn't as composed as he appeared. She watched his fingers smooth down his hair and remembered the brush of his hand on her hair, her cheek, her shoulder. It had taken weeks for her to break down his reserve enough for him to touch her in the casual way that other people do without thinking, and she had treasured his touch the more for that. It had been his reserve, and the elusive sadness she had sensed underneath, that had drawn her to him initially and, in the end, pushed her away.

Now Sam didn't touch her, nor did he give any indication of wanting to. He simply watched her. She might have been a problem in logic that he was trying to work out so he could go on to something else.

"Just living—experiencing—can be painful." A smile touched her lips. "But it's either that or stop living, literally, like poor Freddy, or practically, like a few very unhappy people I've known."

For an instant he dropped his guard and gave her a curiously penetrating smile. "In my business you see more than a few people who're unhappy. What about you, Annie? Are you happy?"

"Absolutely." The question seemed to contain a challenge, and it made her uncomfortable. She moved her shoulders restlessly. "And you?"

"I can't say I've given it much thought," he said softly.

"That's one way of dealing with it," Annie responded. The scent of his after-shave was making her light-headed. She could remember that scent on his skin when they'd made love, how it had mingled with the heady aroma of male sweat and sex. Vivid memories bombarded her, sweet barbs of throat-tightening poignancy.

Oh, how they had made love once the barriers had fallen! Throughout the long winter nights, with the fire blazing on the hearth and snow falling outside. On lazy, rainy mornings and sleepy weekend afternoons. Together they had discovered things about each other that had thrilled and enthralled them. He had made her comfortable with her innately sensual nature, and she had opened the floodgates of his passion. With their bodies they had communicated freely—but only with their bodies, and in the end it hadn't been enough for Annie. She had wanted it all and had ended with nothing.

Heaven help her, she thought frantically, if Sam touched her now....

"So, your life is going well. Are you involved with someone?" He asked the question in a strangely detached tone, as though he were making rather tedious conversation with a seatmate on a plane.

Annie controlled the urge to scream that he had lost the right to question her about anything. "I'm married to my work." She lifted her chin. "I learned that from you."

He scanned her face as though searching for something more. "You always did resent my work."

"That's not true!" She had promised herself that if she ever saw him again, she wouldn't get emotional.

Once she let her feelings loose, there was no telling what kind of fool they would make of her. But caution was overwhelmed by the sting of his unwarranted accusation and the words burst from her, surprising them both. "My God, Sam, didn't you know me at all? After everything that happened between us, how could you not understand me better than that?"

"I thought I understood you," he tossed back, "until I came home and found you'd cleared out without a word. Couldn't you have had the consideration to tell me to my face?"

"Consideration?" She shook her head in furious exasperation. "I don't think you're in any position to call me inconsiderate, Sam." She fought back the hot impulse to say more, much more. "I left because I had to. I won't be made to feel guilty about it, either."

"We were lovers for seven months," he said, still with the same accusing tone.

"I know exactly how long it was."

"And you knew exactly how to hurt me, too, didn't you?" he asked tightly.

"That doesn't even deserve a reply." She struggled with the need to fly at him in helpless rage. Instead she strode toward the closed door in the corner of the room. "It's a quarter after ten. I'm tired of waiting for Smallwood. I wonder if he's even in there."

Before she reached the door, it opened. A balding, heavyset man in an obviously custom-made beige silk suit came into the waiting area. "Sorry to keep you waiting, Miss Malloy, Mr. Bennington." He shook hands with Annie and Sam, adding, "I had an important long-distance call." He rubbed his hands together briskly. "Well, I imagine you two have introduced yourselves."

"Miss Malloy and I have known each other for some time," Sam said without looking at Annie.

"Good, good. Come into my office and sit down, please. This won't take long."

Eager to get the business taken care of and be out of there, Annie strode into the office and the men followed. She and Sam settled in two maroon leather chairs and the attorney sat behind the desk, facing them. "Did you have a pleasant flight?" he inquired of Annie.

"It was fine." Why didn't he get on with it?

"The receptionist can bring us something to drink. Coffee? Tea?"

"Nothing for me, thank you," Annie said.

"I don't care for anything, either," Sam said.

Smallwood looked curiously from Annie to Sam as though sensing the tension between them for the first time. "All right, then." Smallwood picked up a sheet of paper. "Mr. Malloy's will is a simple, direct instrument. One page, as you can see. I'll have copies mailed to both of you, of course. For now I'll skip all the introductory legal jargon. There are some small bequests of personal items, furniture, things like that to a few of Mr. Malloy's business associates here in L.A. I'll skip that, too, and merely read the pertinent paragraph." He cleared his throat theatrically. "'To my cousin, Anne Marie Malloy, and to my boyhood friend, Samuel David Bennington, I leave in equal portions, share and share alike, my most precious possession, my beloved basset hound, California.'"

Smallwood looked up expectantly. "She's called Callie for short."

Annie stared at the attorney's beefy face. Then she darted a glance at Sam, who appeared as stunned as she was. She looked back at Smallwood. "Did you say basset hound?" she asked incredulously.

"That's right, Miss Malloy. My congratulations. Your cousin must have had a great deal of confidence in you and Mr. Bennington to leave Callie to you. I'm sure his confidence wasn't misplaced."

"Freddy left me a *dog*?" Sam seemed to be having trouble taking it in. "Or more precisely, half a dog?"

Annie was still churning with emotions stirred up by her confrontation with Sam in the waiting room. Now she learned she'd flown all the way to L.A. to be told she'd inherited half-ownership of a basset hound!

This must be a dream, she thought crazily. It can't really be happening. Not that she didn't love dogs, she just couldn't keep one in her apartment. *Freddy, I'll kill you!* The irony of the thought struck her suddenly and she had an urge to laugh hysterically. She didn't dare give in to the impulse, though, for fear she wouldn't be able to stop. At the same time, she felt like crying because the only thing Freddy had to leave behind, after thirty-two years, was a dog.

"Callie isn't just any dog, Mr. Bennington." Smallwood sounded a bit miffed. "She's an extremely valuable animal, I dare say one of the most valuable animals in the United States of America."

Annie gaped at Smallwood and realized he was deadly serious. A bark of amazed laughter escaped Sam. "That's nonsense. How valuable can a basset hound be, even a registered one?"

Smallwood gazed at Sam in bewilderment. "Forgive me, Mr. Bennington, I assumed you knew—I assumed everybody knew—who Callie is. Of course, she's registered, but that isn't what makes her so valuable. Why, she's famous. California is the Chow Hound dog."

Annie felt as though she'd arrived in the middle of a complicated movie plot. "What's he talking about, Sam?"

"Wait a minute, I'm finally getting an inkling." Sam sat forward in his chair. "Chow Hound is a brand of dog food, right?"

"The best-selling dog food in the country," Smallwood informed them.

"They advertise on television, right? I don't have time to watch much TV, but I think I saw one of their commercials a few weeks back."

"Then you saw Callie," Smallwood said. "She's the basset hound that does those cute tricks. Mr. Malloy trained her himself. Worked with her all the time. He loved that dog."

"Well, I'll be damned," Sam said. His dazed expression made Annie's lips twitch, in spite of the impossible predicament she found herself in.

"Good for old Freddy," Sam went on. "He finally had an idea that worked." He stared thoughtfully at the will on Smallwood's desk for a moment. "I'm gratified that Freddy thought so highly of me, Mr. Smallwood, but I can't take care of a dog. My work requires that I be away from home for days at a time."

Smallwood looked at Annie. "Perhaps Miss Malloy—"

"No pets are allowed in my apartment complex," Annie put in hastily.

"Well, it seems the two of you have a small problem to work out," Smallwood said blithely. "I'm certain you'll come up with a satisfactory solution." He opened his desk drawer and took out a small sheet of paper. "Now, here's the name and address of the veterinary clinic where Callie has been kenneled since Mr. Malloy's unfortunate accident. I've drawn a little map on the back, showing you how to get there from here." He handed the paper to Annie. Smallwood took out a second slip of paper. "And here's the name and telephone number of Callie's agent, Mr. F. R. Barnes. Mr. Barnes is quite eager to talk with the two of you while you're here. He'll be at that number all day."

Sam was grinning. "Smallwood, are you sitting there with a straight face and telling us Freddy's dog has an agent?"

Smallwood was not amused. "Certainly. Nobody works in the film business in this town without an agent. Mr. Barnes will inform you of the terms of Callie's contract and other necessary business arrangements. I don't mean to rush you, but I'm expected at home for a family gathering."

Now that he'd performed his duty as executor, Smallwood seemed eager to be rid of them. No doubt he was relieved to have Callie off his hands, Annie thought. *Freddy, you knew I'm a sucker for homeless animals.*

Growing up, Annie had made a habit of taking in stray dogs and cats, to her parents' dismay. Her father used to claim that half their grocery bill was spent on dog and cat food. He had bemoaned Annie's zoo, as he called it, every time Freddy and his parents came to visit.

Freddy had known she couldn't turn her back on a homeless dog. He had known Annie would see that Callie was well cared for, somehow. His motives for leaving the dog to Sam and Annie jointly were less pure. Freddy had devised this clever scheme to throw her and Sam together.

"Annie, are you in a state of shock?" Sam was standing beside her chair. "Should we call the paramedics?" Evidently he'd been talking to her and she hadn't heard a word he'd said.

"No, I'm fine," she said, ignoring his sarcasm. She rose from her chair and followed Sam out of the office.

"Shrewd Freddy," Sam muttered close to Annie's ear. "Damn his hide." Sam knew as well as Annie did what Freddy had been up to with his bequest.

"We'll figure out something," Annie said weakly.

"Maybe the agent can keep her," Sam mused. "Give me that paper with his number on it. I'll use the receptionist's phone to call him."

Annie had to run to keep up with his purposeful strides. "We have to meet him before we decide something like that. I couldn't leave her with someone I haven't even laid eyes on."

He answered with a grunt of impatience. "The man's making commissions off the dog. He has a vested interest in taking good care of her."

"I have to meet him," Annie insisted.

Sam recognized the stubborn tilt of her chin and wanted to shake her. But he didn't have the courage to touch her, not in any way. When she'd left him, he'd

promised himself never to be vulnerable again. He'd
had not a single doubt that he was over her until he'd
turned around and seen her standing in Smallwood's
waiting room. Now he had doubts in plenty. He would
conquer them, of course. It was a simple matter of
willpower.

Two
___

Annie stared out the taxi window at a distant snow-capped mountain. She had never been to Southern California before, and the contrasts fascinated her. Where else could you pick an orange from a tree while looking at a snow-covered peak? Where else could you swim in the ocean in the morning, then ski down a snowy mountain in the afternoon?

She didn't like the smog, though, and traveling on the freeways made her hair stand on end.

Sam sat beside her in the back seat, staring out the opposite window. They were going to meet Callie's agent for lunch in an Italian restaurant on Melrose Avenue in Hollywood.

Being with Sam continued to stir sweet, bitter memories in Annie, memories she thought she'd laid to rest long ago.

She had heard Freddy talk about his friend, Sam, for years before she ever met him. Two years ago she'd accompanied Freddy to a bookstore, browsing while he looked for books on commodity trading. Freddy was suffering from one of his periodic brainstorms; this one had to do with making a fast fortune in soybean futures. A few weeks later Freddy had scraped together five thousand dollars, most of it borrowed from friends. He'd bought a ninety-day option, betting that the price of soybeans would go up. Instead the price went down and Freddy had lost the money, along with his dream of becoming a hotshot commodities trader.

That day in the bookstore, Annie had been leafing through a new novel by her favorite author when Freddy found her and dragged her away from the mystery section. "Sam Bennington just came into the store," Freddy said. "I've wanted to introduce you two for ages."

In fact Freddy had tried to get her and his friend Sam together for dinner a few weeks before that, but Annie had evaded her cousin's matchmaking efforts. She had recently ended an unsatisfactory relationship, the second in as many years, and had concluded that she might never again feel up to a serious involvement.

The problem was that she seemed to be drawn to the wrong kind of men. Twice she had drifted into relationships where she played a nurturing role. She would start out wanting to help a man "find himself" and end up feeling used. Perhaps this distressing tendency was a carryover from her years of bringing home stray animals.

At any rate, that day in the bookstore she wasn't interested in meeting any new men. Unfortunately there was no way to avoid being introduced to Freddy's friend, so she pasted a smile on her face and tried to accept the inevitable with good grace.

Sam Bennington was so different from the previous men in Annie's life that he might have been from another planet. He knew exactly who he was and where he was going. His work with one of Oklahoma City's large law firms engrossed him, and outside of working hours, he was a loner. He owned twenty acres west of the city and planned to build a house there with his own hands, using skills he'd learned on summer construction jobs during his college and law school years. He drew endless floor plans and spent hours walking alone over his acreage, content with his own company.

According to Freddy, Sam had dated several women through the years, but Sam had always ended the relationships before a commitment was made. It was Freddy's conviction that Sam simply hadn't "met the right woman," yet.

Sam was the most independent, self-sufficient man Annie had ever known. The first few times Sam asked her out, she was certain that he was doing it only to placate Freddy; Sam Bennington didn't need anybody but himself.

Looking back, she realized that she must have already been half in love with Sam when she'd walked out of the bookstore with Freddy that day. By the time Sam brought her home from their first date, her heart was hopelessly lost. She had managed to hide the fact from everybody except herself, but she lived for their times together, unable to say no to his invitations even as she struggled with the premonition that Sam would break her heart.

Miraculously he seemed to enjoy her company, and slowly she sensed his reserve thawing. He was a puzzle and a challenge to her. He never talked about his past and changed the subject whenever Annie brought it up. The little Annie knew about Sam's past she'd learned from Freddy. Sam's parents had been divorced when he was quite young and he'd stayed with his father. Then, after his father died when Sam was in his early teens, Sam had lived with foster families until he was eighteen. He'd put himself through college and law school while maintaining an almost straight-A average. Freddy didn't know what had become of Sam's mother.

If Annie had deliberately set out to find a man who was her opposite in almost every way, she'd have picked Sam. He was the epitome of the strong, silent type. He kept his feelings under tight control and it wasn't easy for him to share his deepest thoughts. Annie wanted to talk about everything, and sparks of emotion shot out of her at the slightest provocation.

Sam's approach to life was organized. His office and house were squeaky clean, as neat as military barracks. Annie was impulsive, rarely planning anything ahead of time. Her office and apartment were clean enough, but invariably cluttered. She acknowledged that "a place for everything and everything in its place" was a wonderful concept, but it simply didn't work for her. She was usually in too much of a hurry to put things away when she was finished with them. Rather, she went on clean-up binges two or

three times a year whenever the clutter became un-
manageable.

Because she was in love with Sam, she accepted him
as he was—or tried to. She even thought he was falling in love with her, too. In bed, he let down all the
barriers. Their lovemaking was wild and passionate.
Annie told herself that eventually he would open up to
her in other ways, as well.

Now, as she rode with Sam to meet the agent, the
memories were so strong that even the tastes and
smells and sounds came back. Running across Sam's
rural acreage, hand in hand, with the wind in her face
and the smell of burning leaves in her nostrils. Warm
flesh and wet mouths in dim bedrooms. Laughing at
everything and nothing. Turning herself inside out for
him; wanting all of him in return and being denied it.
Growing frustration. Desperation. Heartbreak.

"I have a feeling," Sam muttered, "that no matter
what Barnes says, you won't be willing to fly out of
here without that dog."

His words snapped Annie out of the past. "I know
you don't want to do this, Sam, but must you be such
a poor sport about it?"

"This isn't a tennis game."

"Pity. If it were, you could go home, put your
racket in a closet and forget about it. It takes a little
more thought to decide what to do with a dog."

"I know you, Annie. You want to take that dog
home with us."

"It's what Freddy wanted."

"Wrong. What Freddy wanted was to put me in a
damned embarrassing predicament. Wherever he is

right now, I'll bet he's watching me squirm, and laughing.''

Being with her *embarrassed* him! And he had no compunction about telling her so. Annie counted silently to ten before she said, ''Look, Sam. I'm not any happier about this situation than you are, but we own the dog. We have to decide together what to do with her.''

''Hah! You and I have rarely agreed on anything. Freddy knew that, dammit.''

''We'll just have to put our personal feelings aside while we work this out,'' she said stiffly.

''Right.'' There was mockery and a faint threat in the twist of his lips. Annie clasped her hands primly in her lap. She felt Sam studying her and stared out the taxi window, seeing nothing.

The agent was a nervous, chain-smoking little man with a face ruddied by heavy drinking and a mop of bleached blond hair. He sat at a corner table, smoking a second cigarette—the stub of the first lay in an ashtray near his hand. A waiter pointed out Barnes to Sam and Annie. Barnes jumped up as they approached—like a puppet on a string, Annie thought.

''Hi, there!'' Barnes wore a billowy white shirt, open at the neck to reveal a red ascot, and black trousers with pleats at the waist and narrow ankles. He bounced on the heels of his black patent-leather loafers as he shook their hands. ''I'm Froslich Barnes.'' He made a gagging gesture. ''It's a family name. I'll never forgive my mother for hanging it on me. Everybody calls me Frosty.'' He bounded around the table to hold Annie's chair for her. "Do sit down, darling."

The use of the meaningless endearment scraped along Annie's nerve endings. She hid her face behind a menu. While Sam and Annie perused the menu, Barnes lit another cigarette and sucked it greedily between suggestions as to what they should order. Barnes chose spaghetti with mushroom sauce. Annie decided on lasagne, and Sam on fettuccine. A waiter poured red wine into their glasses.

"Well, well," said Barnes, beaming at them as though they were two obedient children who had pleased him. He lifted his glass. "Here's to show biz. I imagine you two were a bit startled to learn you'd inherited a basset hound who makes TV commercials."

Sam, who had disliked the man on sight, went straight to the business at hand. "Mr. Smallwood said you could enlighten us about the agreement with the dog food company. Exactly what are the terms of the contract?"

Barnes downed his wine, then waved his cigarette. "It's your standard contract—five-figure advances, royalties, residuals. Spells out how the arrangements for the tapings will be made, how the tapings will be handled, et cetera, et cetera, et cetera."

"How much money does it come to?" Annie asked.

"Honey, that's the question every agent wishes he could answer." Ashes from Barnes's cigarette dropped on the white tablecloth and he brushed at them impatiently. "No way of knowing what it'll come to in any six-month period until the statements come in."

He grinned. "But let's face it, we're not talking about Lassie here."

"Based on past statements," Sam said, "give us a ball-park figure."

Barnes shrugged helplessly. "Well, the advance money on the current contract is long gone. Freddy was a big spender, as I'm sure you two know. Royalties depend on how many tapings are made and how many times the commercials are shown."

"What did Callie earn last year?" Sam persisted.

"Now I'd have to check my books to get close, Sam. You don't mind if I call you Sam, do you? Let's just say that Callie has been earning decent money, but you ain't gonna retire in the lap of luxury any time soon."

"Mr. Barnes—" Annie began.

"Frosty, please. I'll get you those figures later. Okay?" He rested his elbows on the table and leaned toward them confidentially. "Right now, I'm much more concerned about having Callie available for tapings. They can call for one at any time, you know. I assume both of you are gainfully employed?" He grinned like a fool but didn't wait for an answer. "Then neither of you can hop on a plane with Callie any old time on twenty-four hours' notice."

Their food arrived. Barnes emptied his wineglass for the second time and called for a refill. "I'll just tell you what I have in mind," he said. "You turn Callie over to me, and I'll find a good kennel and a good trainer for her. Those little tricks she does have to be continually reinforced, you know. I'd recommend Brad Delano in Bel Air. He's—"

"Mr. Barnes," Sam interrupted.

"Frosty."

"Frosty," Sam pronounced with great precision. "The contract must spell out how many tapings Callie is expected to make. How many is that?"

"Well—two a year. But a taping can take days before they get it right. Callie's cute, but she is a dumb animal."

"I just don't think we can make this decision right now," Annie put in. "I'm sure you understand, Mr.—er, Frosty." She half expected Sam to contradict her, but he had turned his attention to his meal and said nothing.

"Then you'll be staying in L.A. for a few days?" Barnes asked.

"That's not possible," Sam said. "We can probably let you know our decision later today."

"Well, uh, it's essential that we get Callie on Delano's waiting list as soon as possible...."

Both Annie and Sam looked at Barnes without comment. He sputtered some more, then attacked his spaghetti. Sam deliberately turned the conversation to the California weather. Looking pained, Barnes murmured monosyllabic replies.

"We'll get back to you," Sam said a while later as he and Annie rose to leave.

"You have my number."

"By the way," Sam said, as though it were an afterthought, "we'll be requesting an audit of your records of California's earnings. You'll be hearing from Mr. Smallwood on that." Sam fished a business card out of his pocket and handed it to Barnes. "And I'd like to have a copy of the contract with the dog food company as well as one of the agreement between you and Freddy."

"If you insist, but—"

Sam's brows rose quizzically. "Is this a problem for you, Frosty?"

Barnes was staring at the business card. "You're a lawyer?" he sputtered. "Uh, no problem."

"Good. We'll be expecting to receive the contracts from you in a few days. Ready, Annie?"

"Yes. Thank you for lunch, Mr. Barnes." The agent was ordering another bottle of wine as they left.

Sam hailed a taxi outside the restaurant and gave the driver the address of the kennel. When they were on the way, Sam muttered, "Barnes is a con man."

Annie was relieved to hear that. At least they agreed on something. "I wouldn't trust him any farther than I could throw him," she said fervently.

"He's probably been stealing Freddy blind."

"How will we prevent his doing the same to us?"

"I don't know yet. Let's wait until we see those contracts."

"I know one thing," Annie said. "I couldn't live with myself if I left Callie in that man's clutches."

Sam, who was gazing morosely at the back of the driver's head, didn't respond. Annie studied his profile, looking for a sign that his determination to leave Callie in L.A. was weakening.

"Two tapings a year isn't so bad," she ventured.

He grunted.

"I'm not even sure we need a trainer," Annie plowed ahead. "After all, Callie already knows the tricks. All we have to do is put her through her paces regularly."

Sam gave her a long-suffering look. "We?"

"It wouldn't kill you," Annie said dryly.

At the veterinary clinic they introduced themselves to the young woman at the desk and explained why they were there. Connie Valdez seemed glad to see them. "We've been expecting you. Mr. Smallwood called to tell us you were coming." She led them to the kennels behind the clinic. "Callie's in the pen at the end of this row." When they reached it, she added, "She's in the doghouse. Callie, come on out, girl."

The dog got slowly to her feet and, head drooping, long ears dragging along the ground, plodded over to the fence. Her coloring was liver and white with circles of black hair around a pair of the saddest brown eyes Annie had ever seen.

"Oh, Sam, look at her," Annie cried. She unlatched the gate and, kneeling, wrapped her arms around the dog. "Poor baby," she crooned. "You miss Freddy, don't you?"

Callie licked her cheek and whined pitifully.

"We've been a little worried about her," Mrs. Valdez said. "She's been awfully depressed the last couple of weeks."

"Don't you worry, Callie," Annie soothed. "We're taking you home with us. Aren't we, Sam?"

Watching Annie hug the dog, Sam saw that further objection would be useless. He knew how stubborn Annie could be when her heart was engaged, and she'd given her heart to that dog the instant she saw her. He had no idea what they'd do with Callie once they reached Oklahoma City. Nor had Annie, he was sure.

"I'm so glad to hear that," Mrs. Valdez said. "Callie's a sweetheart, aren't you, girl?"

Callie managed a halfhearted wag of her tail as Annie scratched behind her ears. For a crazy instant Sam wished he was the object of all that crooning and petting. He pulled himself up short. They'd better get to the airport and arrange for Callie's flight, since Annie was dead set on taking her. Resigned, he said, "I'll go settle the bill."

At the airport Annie came close to tears when Callie was confined in a carrier for the flight. "I wish I could keep her with me," she wailed.

"They won't allow it," Sam said. "Come on, it's time to board."

Abruptly, Annie was diverted by the touch of Sam's hand at the small of her back as he guided her down the boarding tunnel. Heat jolted through her and her insides turned to jelly. Dear Lord, it felt good to be touched by Sam again.

Sam's hand had drifted to the small of Annie's back without conscious volition. It was reflex, a habit remembered from their months together. He had never been a toucher until Annie came into his life, but in seven months he hadn't been able to get enough of touching her.

The second he realized what he'd done, he jerked his hand away. Why was it that with Annie, and only Annie, his control was perpetually in danger of slipping? He stuffed the offending hand into his trouser pocket and stood back for her to enter the plane ahead of him. It gave him bitter pleasure to see the erratic jump of pulse at the base of her throat as she brushed past him.

For just an instant, when Sam jerked his hand away, Annie had seen confusion in his eyes. She wondered what it meant but clamped down on the thought. His touch had been accidental, that was obvious. Sam hadn't *wanted* to touch her in more than a year.

Annie let Sam sit next to the window and buckled herself into the center seat. An elderly man, with his head buried in the *Wall Street Journal*, had the aisle seat. Annie put her head back and closed her eyes.

Covertly, Sam let his gaze scan Annie's serene face. Her moods were like quicksilver. She had gone from tearful anxiety over Callie to perfect composure, at least on the surface. For an insane moment he wanted to shake her. It wasn't the first time that day he'd had the urge, he recalled. Annie had always had the ability to confuse his neat, logical thought processes.

At the moment the impulse to shake her was being crowded out by even more unsettling urges. He wanted to taste her mouth again—to smash through the control rebuilt over fifteen empty months with one long, hungry kiss. Desire was suddenly a hot pain in his groin and a breathless panic in his chest. He clenched his teeth and fought himself, hating his own weakness. He grabbed a magazine from the seat pocket in front of him, opened it and started reading. But he couldn't make any sense of the words.

Annie pretended to nap while she tried to sort out her thoughts. Why hadn't she pulled away from Sam's touch before he removed his hand? She'd been enjoying it too much, that's why! How could she be such a sap? Hadn't she learned her lesson the first time? Groaning inwardly, she hauled her thoughts to Callie, now riding in a cramped carrier in the plane's baggage section. She must be feeling abandoned—again. Annie was determined not to take her to another kennel in Oklahoma City.

She opened her eyes and caught Sam watching her, but she couldn't tell what he was thinking. Well, wasn't she used to that? She stirred restlessly. "Do you still live in the same apartment?"

"No." He took his time studying her face. "I moved into my house six months ago. Four of the rooms are livable, and I'm working on the rest as I can."

Annie fought off memories of pouring over blueprints with Sam, his arm flung over her shoulders, loving the excitement in his voice as he described the house he wanted to build. "You built in the country?"

"Dead center of my twenty acres." After Annie left, building the house had saved his sanity. He would lose himself in the physical labor for hours at a time. His hands had grown tough with calluses and his muscles had hardened, along with his heart.

Annie cocked her head. "With a deck on the east so you can watch the sunrise. I remember. Do you have a fenced yard?"

Sam's eyes narrowed. "Yes, and I know what you're thinking, Annie. It won't work. I don't need a dog in my life."

Her brown eyes blazed with sudden anger. "Tell me something I don't know, Sam," she fired back. "I'm well aware that you don't *need* anything or anybody. But there's nowhere else for Callie to go. All you'd have to do is get a doghouse and give her food and water daily. Surely that won't take up too much of your valuable time."

He had a rein on his emotions now. As usual, she was charging ahead on impulse, not considering all the ramifications. "What about her training? Who's going to do that?"

"I will. I can drive out and work with her a couple of days a week. And I'll be responsible for visits to the vet, and whatever else has to be done."

Stubborn. That was the only word for Annie when she got a bee in her bonnet. "In the first place, I'm scheduled to fly to Houston tomorrow evening and I won't be back until Wednesday afternoon."

"Oh." The passionate gleam in her eyes faltered for a moment. "We can't just dump her at your place and take off before she has a chance to get used to it."

"As I was saying, I can't—"

Impulsively she touched the back of his hand where it rested on the metal arm between them. A light brush of her fingertips before she seemed to realize what she'd done and pulled away. Sam had to grip the hard metal to keep from turning his hand over and enveloping her hand.

"Here's what we'll do," Annie exclaimed. "I'll hide Callie in my apartment until Wednesday. Then I can drive her out to your house Wednesday after work."

"You really think you can conceal Callie for four days? You'll have to take her out for walks. And what if she barks while you're at work?"

"Darn it, Sam! Will you stop shooting holes in every suggestion I make? If you have a better idea, let's hear it. Only don't bring up leaving her in a kennel. I simply can't do it."

Sam threw up his hands in defeat. "All right, all right. We'll try it your way and see how it goes."

Annie leaned back in her seat. Her smile was a bit smug. "Thank you, Sam."

* * *

"Hurry up," Sam muttered. "She weighs a ton."

Callie was draped over Sam's shoulder, her ears hanging down his back, her sad eyes watching Annie's every move. "Shh," Annie cautioned. "Somebody will hear us." Suppressing a giggle, she unlocked her front door.

They went in and Annie closed the door hastily. Sam dropped Callie on the couch. "You're forty pounds of dead weight, Callie, and your hide's too loose to get a good hold on you." The dog crawled on her belly to the edge of the couch, put her head down and covered her eyes with her paws. She looked for all the world as though she'd been caught doing something naughty and was trying to hide behind her paws.

Annie laughed delightedly. "Look, Sam. Isn't that cute?"

"Cute."

"Don't be sarcastic."

He shrugged. "It's one of her tricks. A conditioned response to some stimulus."

"What stimulus?"

Callie lifted her head and cocked it to one side, watching them expectantly. "Must have been what I said," Sam suggested. "Something about her being forty pounds of dead weight."

Callie kept watching them intently.

"And then you said her hide was loose," Annie said. Callie promptly did her trick again. "Hide!" Annie exclaimed. "That's it. She thought you were telling her to hide." She scratched behind Callie's ears. Callie lifted her head and licked Annie's hand. "Good girl. You see, Sam? She's going to be easy to work with."

"Seems so," he murmured in agreement. His gaze drifted idly around the room. Annie had lived in a different apartment when he'd met her, but this one had the same cluttered appearance as the previous one. A red sweater was draped over the back of the chair. The toes of a pair of white tennis shoes protruded from beneath the couch. Several file folders were scattered over the desk, surrounding an empty plate and a half-full cup of stale coffee.

Automatically, Sam picked up the dishes and carried them to the sink in the adjoining kitchen. Annie was grinning when he came back into the room. "Still Mr. Clean, huh?"

He smiled sheepishly. "Yeah, and you're still... Annie." All at once he felt claustrophobic. Too close to Annie for comfort. He wandered restlessly toward the door but stopped before reaching it. "Do you want me to walk Callie before I go?"

Annie looked at him in surprise. "That's very considerate of you, Sam. But I can do it later." He seemed suddenly uneasy with her, but surely she was misreading him. More likely, he was impatient to be gone.

She walked over to him. Oddly there was a feeling of expectancy in the air, like a wire drawn taut. *Oh, Sam, if only you could have let me in.* "Would you like something to eat before you leave?"

He hesitated before he shook his head. "No, thanks."

Annie was suddenly nervous. She moved to open the door for him. In doing so, she brushed against him, her breasts skimming over his arm. She felt him stiffen and looked up at him as warmth rushed up her neck and into her face. "I'm sorry.... I—"

She knew it was going to happen before he moved, and she did nothing to stop it. Later she would castigate herself for her weakness. But in that moment all she could do was stare at him.

"Damn you, Annie," he groaned. Then his arms came around her and his mouth crushed hers. Everything, including the past fifteen months, melted away under the greedy onslaught of his mouth.

Three

Annie wasn't sure when the punishing kiss turned into a slow, gentle exploration. It was like the first time he'd kissed her, his mouth warm and tender and sweetly yearning. It amazed her now as it had then that such a strong, self-sufficient man could be so gentle.

As she had the first time, she became lost in the heady warmth of his mouth. No man had ever kissed her as Sam did, and perhaps that was why she was incapable of stopping it. Annie would fight force like a tiger, but she was enslaved by tenderness, mesmerized by the hard, male need held in check by Sam's gentle kiss. When he uttered a low-throated groan and drew her closer, her fingers clutched handfuls of his shirt convulsively. Oh, Lord, it felt so right to be kissing Sam again.

Overriding his hunger and masculine drive, Sam's lovemaking had been touched with patience and intricate care, as though he'd wanted Annie to derive as much pleasure from it as he. It had always been that way with Sam. When he made love to her, he made her feel as though she were the loveliest, most desirable woman in the world. Heady stuff. What woman could resist? Certainly not Annie. And now it didn't even occur to her to try. She simply let go and lost herself, sinking into the kiss. All she could think of was how desperately she'd missed Sam's kisses.

Her fingers, which still clutched his shirt, relaxed and her hands crept inside his jacket and under his arms until her palms flattened against his back. She felt the heat of his skin and the hardness of muscle beneath his shirt. Urgently, she pressed closer and her fingers dug into his back.

No one but Sam had ever made her feel such rich, greedy passion. All the old needs—to experience everything that a woman could know with a man, to dive to the core of Sam's carefully controlled passion, to share with him the exquisite pleasure that she had known with no other man—rose up in Annie as if she had never banished them.

It had been too long! She had grown so accustomed to being alone, to the emptiness of her personal life, that she had forgotten the joy of being in Sam's arms, the glory of giving herself without restraint. Sometimes, during the past fifteen months, she had dreamed of knowing these feelings once more. Perhaps this was just another dream. But if so, she never wanted it to be over. She didn't think she could face the dark, cold emptiness of waking alone in her bed and knowing that it hadn't really happened. She denied the possibility that she was dreaming with a moan of protest and pressed against him.

Sam had never meant to touch her. When she'd accidentally brushed against him, he'd had every intention of stepping around her and going out the door. How, then, had he ended up with his arms wrapped around Annie and her soft, warm, feminine body pressing hard against him and setting off shock waves in his bloodstream?

He couldn't remember how it had happened. He knew only that once he'd started kissing her, sharp-edged hunger sliced through reason and defenses, crowding everything else from his mind. Need so strong it left room for nothing else demolished pride, self-protection, common sense—whatever was in its path.

No other woman had ever made him *need* her like this. He hated the vulnerability that such need created, but he hadn't the strength to rid himself of it. Through the sheer power of his will, he had demolished his childhood need for parents, a family. And he thought he'd freed himself of his need for Annie. He'd been wrong.

Even as he despised his own weakness, he wanted to take her right there on the carpet, heedless of the consequences. His bed and his life had been empty for too long. Yet, until today when he saw Annie again, he hadn't known. She had ripped away the facade of his prized self-sufficiency and made him recognize his need for her.

Only a shred of satisfaction could be salvaged from the cataclysm of old feelings released by the kiss—she wanted him, too. She was soft and eager in his arms, her mouth as greedy as his. She wanted him, but she had left him. *Why? Oh, Annie, why?*

Something wet and insistent pushed against Annie's knee, and she murmured a soft protest against Sam's lips. Then Callie whined, and Annie identified the wet, insistent object as the dog's nose. She tried to ignore it, but Callie pushed harder; she must need to go outside.

Sam must have become aware of Callie, too, for he lifted his head slowly. Dazed and disoriented, Annie stared up at him. Their gazes met, and in those first few moments, Sam's gray eyes were the color of slate, as tumultuous as a storm at sea. Then the shades came down.

Her eyes were wide and as dark as midnight. Her soft, full lips were moist and slightly parted, her breathing quick and erratic. She had always looked this way when they'd made love. This was how he'd remembered her after she left him, the way he saw her every time he closed his eyes. That look had kept him awake countless nights, haunted his dreams when he finally did sleep and driven him to the edge of sanity.

Desire, as searing as a hot iron, curled in upon itself like a fist of flame in his gut. A belated resurgence of self-protection gave him the strength to step back and well away from her.

"That was a mistake—I'm sorry—I . . ." He swallowed a mumbled oath. He was stammering! He felt like an utter fool. Not trusting himself to say anything more, he jerked open the door and walked out.

Annie stared at the closed door, wondering for one crazy instant if she'd imagined Sam's being there, kissing her. Callie nudged her wet nose into her hand. Annie patted the dog's head absently and turned away from the door.

Of course, she hadn't imagined it. Sam had been there, and he'd kissed her. Then he'd said it was all a mistake, mumbled something that had sounded like a curse and walked out without another word. Sam Bennington hadn't changed a bit! Annie still couldn't tell what was going on in his head. She'd certainly had no inkling that he was thinking about kissing her until he'd grabbed her and pulled her roughly into his arms.

For a few moments then, she had been in heaven. When Sam had started kissing her, she'd forgotten her reasons for leaving him, forgotten the promises she'd made to herself over the past fifteen months, and kissed him back. Eagerly. She had no idea how it had happened, but it had and she couldn't deny it. What was worse, she wasn't sure she'd have the strength to do things differently if she could live the moment over again.

Annie sighed aloud, and Callie whined, nuzzling Annie's hand again. "Do you want to go out, girl? Okay. We'll go to the store and buy dog food."

Annie snapped on the leash she'd bought at the veterinary clinic in L.A., slid her feet into a pair of comfortable loafers, grabbed her purse and stuck her head out the door to see if any of her neighbors were around.

She was surprised to see that darkness had fallen while she was forgetting herself in Sam's arms. But the exterior of the apartment building was well lighted, and no one was in sight. Annie tugged on Callie's leash. Needing no further encouragement, Callie bounded outside and dragged Annie down the walk.

"Slow down, Callie," Annie whispered.

The dog lunged aside to sniff a bush near the walk. "Okay," Annie whispered. "We'll run to the store. I guess you need it after being cooped up for so long. But we walk back."

Fortunately there was a convenience store only three blocks away. Annie tied Callie's leash to a bicycle rack near the door. "Stay," she said. Callie seemed to understand, for she sat down instantly and cocked her head at Annie.

Annie bought a sack of Chow Hound dog food and returned to find Callie sitting on the same spot where she'd left her. "Good dog," Annie approved as she untied the leash. Clearly, Freddy had trained Callie well.

Back in the apartment she poured dog food into a plastic bowl and filled another with water. The dog lapped water thirstily, and Annie left her to eat while she made toast, bacon and scrambled eggs for herself.

When she carried her meal to the kitchen table, though, Callie padded at her heels. After sniffing at the dog food and turning up her nose, Callie had evidently decided to sit beside Annie's chair and beg for whatever Annie was having.

"You can look so pitiful," Annie told her. Callie watched closely as Annie took each bite. She made Annie feel so guilty that Annie ended up giving half of her meal to Callie. "Too persnickety to eat dog food, I guess," Annie said. Callie licked the plate clean and looked up at Annie happily, her tongue flopping out one side of her mouth. "I hope word doesn't get out that you won't touch Chow Hound," Annie said, laughing. She fondled the dog's ears. "Feeding you could get expensive, California."

Before getting ready for bed, Annie discovered other commands in addition to "Hide" and "Stay." Callie also responded to "Lie down," "Beg" and "Shake hands." She suspected the dog would respond to "Speak," too, but was afraid to try it. One of the neighbors might hear Callie barking.

Annie made a bed for the dog in the kitchen, but Callie made it clear she preferred the foot of Annie's bed. Annie crumpled under Callie's pitiful look and let her stay. She switched off the light and crawled into bed, scooting Callie to one side with her feet. "You're spoiled rotten, California, and I'm a marshmallow," she mumbled as she tried to find a comfortable position. Annie wondered if she was setting a bad precedent by letting Callie sleep on her bed. Probably, but she was too tired to be a disciplinarian tonight.

Callie fell asleep almost instantly, but Annie lay awake for a long time. Her thoughts kept returning to Sam and the kiss that had started out angry and punishing but quickly changed to a sensitive lover's kiss. The mere memory of the kiss made Annie tremble and pull the sheet closer around her. She hadn't had a relationship with a man since she broke up with Sam, and it had been too long since she'd been kissed. Besides, Sam took her by surprise. Maybe that explained her explosive reaction.

Eventually she fell asleep. Some time before dawn she dreamed that Sam was making love to her, his strong hands roaming over her body and touching all of the sensitive places that Sam alone knew so well. Annie awoke bathed in perspiration, her heart pounding furiously.

Groaning, she sat up and pushed the sheet back. "Freddy, this is all your fault," she muttered. "Why did you do this to me?"

Callie licked Annie's hand in sympathy.

Annie left work at five o'clock Monday afternoon, anxious to get home and check on Callie. The dog had a few rather uncaninelike ideas—such as refusing to eat dog food and an aversion to sleeping on the floor— but otherwise, Annie couldn't have asked for a more considerate houseguest. Callie hadn't barked all weekend, except when Annie took her out for a run Sunday night and Callie saw another dog. Still, Annie felt a bit uneasy all day Monday at the office, wondering what Callie was doing in her absence.

Callie met her at the door, her tail swinging madly. She jumped on Annie to greet her, but one "Down" was all it took to remind her of her manners. The apartment looked exactly as Annie had left it. Callie hadn't even bothered the tennis shoes peeking from beneath the couch.

Annie shrugged off her jacket and hugged the dog, complimenting her effusively. It was amazing how fond she was of Callie already. Parting with her on Wednesday was going to be hard. Leaving her at Sam's was the only acceptable alternative, though. Every day that Callie stayed in the apartment increased the odds of somebody finding out and reporting her.

The telephone rang and Annie experienced a stab of alarm. Was the game up already? Perhaps Callie had disturbed the neighbors while Annie was at work. She'd say she left her TV on when she went to work that morning, she decided. With a little luck, they might believe her. Reluctantly, Annie flopped down on the couch and picked up the receiver.

"Annie, it's Sam."

The sound of his voice threw Annie into a moment of stunned silence. Gripping the receiver to her ear, she sat as still as a stone. She was oblivious to Callie's head pushing into her lap and asking to be petted. Why was Sam calling her? And how could the mere sound of his voice make her remember so many things that she had sworn to forget and make her want him so desperately? She could actually taste his mouth. She moistened her lips with the tip of her tongue and swallowed hard.

She was too flustered to think of anything sensible to say. "Sam?" was all she could manage.

"I wanted to let you know my plane is scheduled to land in Oklahoma City at six Wednesday evening. I should reach my place by seven-thirty, if you want to bring Callie out then."

He sounded very businesslike. Annie's shoulders sagged under the weight of her disappointment. Sam just wanted to make arrangements about Callie. Of course. What had she expected? "I might wait until Thursday afternoon to bring her. I kind of like having her around."

"She's not causing any problems, then?"

"No—no. She's good company and so lovable. She *is* a bit spoiled, but she's obedient." Annie realized she was rambling to hide her confusion, but she couldn't seem to stop. "She's a big fraud, though. She insists

on eating people food. Won't touch Chow Hound dog
food. How do you suppose they get her to eat it on
TV?"

"Probably lace it with ground sirloin," Sam suggested.

"Yes, probably—uh—" Annie seemed to have run
out of chitchat. She searched frantically for something else to say.

Sam saved her the trouble. "I've been thinking
about what to do with Callie when I have to be out of
town. I have a neighbor, Jude Preston, who's a dog
lover. He took early retirement, so he's home all the
time. I'm sure he'll be glad to look after Callie whenever I need him."

"Oh, well isn't that nice?" Was this Sam's less-
than-subtle way of letting her know that there would
be no reason for her to be running out to his house
frequently?

"I'm glad you haven't had any problems with Callie. Maybe your landlord won't find out, after all."

"So far, so good," Annie murmured.

"I have to go now," Sam said. "I'm meeting a
client for dinner."

Annie felt depressed when she hung up. Absurd, she
told herself. Sam had merely wanted to check with her
about Callie. She'd bet *he* hadn't lain awake thinking
about that kiss. He'd probably put it out of his mind
as soon as he left her apartment. Damn Sam Bennington and his willpower.

"Fine," Annie said out loud. "If that's the way you
want it, Sam, it's fine with me." Callie looked up at
her inquiringly. Annie laughed and stroked the dog's
head. "Don't worry, Callie. I don't intend to aban-

don you to Sam. I don't need Sam's permission to visit you. You're my dog, too, aren't you, girl?''

Laying her cheek against Callie's smooth head, Annie had a sudden inexplicable urge to weep.

Annie worked late Tuesday. When she arrived home at seven, Callie was waiting at the door, wanting to go out for her evening walk. "Give me a few minutes to catch my breath first," Annie pleaded as she dropped her purse and some account folders on the desk. "I'd like to have a cold drink before we go," she told Callie, who still sat gazing longingly at the door. "I'll hurry," Annie promised and went to the kitchen.

As she dropped ice cubes into a glass and poured cola over them, she heard Callie pacing back and forth in front of the door. Such restlessness was unusual. Up to now Callie had seemed perfectly content. Freddy must have had a yard for her, Annie mused. Callie probably wasn't getting enough exercise, and that was all the more reason for her to stay with Sam. Annie knew it had to be, but she didn't have to like it. She was going to miss Callie terribly.

She drank the cola and changed her high heels for comfortable loafers before leaving the apartment complex as furtively as was possible with Callie leaping ahead and dragging Annie at a trot.

Since Callie seemed overjoyed to be outside, Annie let the dog have her lead until they were more than a mile from the apartment. Callie zigged and zagged down and across streets until Annie felt like a ricocheting ball. Finally even Callie was too tired to keep up that pace. She slowed to a walk and plodded along on her big, splayed feet with her tongue lolling out. At that point Annie reversed their direction and they headed back home.

On a quiet, residential street, Annie drew in a deep breath of evening air laden with the scent of honeysuckle. "After that run, we should both sleep well tonight, Callie," she told the dog. "Don't you think so?"

Callie looked back at Annie, then startled Annie by lifting her nose to the sky and howling like a banshee.

"Gracious, what brought that on?"

Callie hung her head and plodded toward home.

"I hope you aren't sick," Annie worried out loud. But Callie had run full speed ahead for a mile. She couldn't do that if she were sick, could she?

Back at the apartment Annie cooked ground beef with chopped onion in a skillet. She removed Callie's portion of the meat before adding spaghetti, cheese and tomato sauce to her own and creating a simple, tasty dish that her mother called "Oklahoma goulash." Together with a green salad and toast spread with melted garlic butter, it made a hearty meal.

Callie ate only half of the meat in her dish before she began pacing restlessly around the apartment. Her toenails clicked rhythmically on the kitchen linoleum. Every time she passed the table where Annie was eating, she stopped to look up at Annie and whine mournfully. Her whines seemed to get louder and louder.

"No!" Annie cautioned, placing her finger to her lips. "You have to be quiet, Callie." Callie looked at her and whined again. "Silence," Annie tried. "Be silent." The dog whined again and walked off. Annie heard her in the living room, scratching at the door.

She went in and ordered Callie to sit. The dog obeyed instantly, but every few minutes she whined piteously. "What is wrong with you?" Annie asked. She was beginning to feel frantic. If Callie kept this up, one of the neighbors was bound to hear her and report Annie.

Annie gave Callie a bowl of milk, which she lapped at a few times before losing interest. Callie wandered around the apartment, sniffing in corners. Annie took a shower and donned a gown and robe. She tried to work on the accounts she'd brought home, but Callie kept planting a paw on Annie's lap and looking up at her pleadingly.

Finally, Annie gave up trying to work and let Callie lie on the couch beside her. She petted and talked to the dog soothingly. "What's wrong, girl? Do you still miss Freddy? Oh, I know—I miss him, too. Freddy was one of a kind. But you have me now, and I love you."

Callie calmed down and even dozed for a while. Annie eased off the couch and returned to her desk. A few minutes later Callie leaped off the couch and let out a bloodcurdling howl.

Annie started violently. "Oh, Callie, what is your problem?" She grabbed Callie's collar and dragged her to the bathroom. "I don't like to do this, but you'll have to stay in here if you can't keep quiet. Lie down. Stay." Annie closed the door and held her breath.

Just as Annie was thinking that Callie's presence in the apartment had gone unnoticed, there was a knock at the door. She knew before she opened the door that her illicit houseguest had been detected. The caller was her landlord.

"Good evening, Mr. Stigler."

Stigler was an elderly bachelor who wore a perpetual scowl on his wizened face. He seemed to be mad at the world. People in the apartment complex referred to him as "The Grouch" behind his back.

"I've had three complaints in the last ten minutes about the noise coming out of this apartment," Stigler snapped, scowling more than usual. "Mrs. Denison says she heard a bloodcurdling howl. Either you've murdered somebody or you have a dog in there, Miss Malloy. Which is it?"

"Well, uh…" At that moment a muffled howl came from the bathroom and Stigler's eyebrows shot up.

"Aha! A dog!" he accused.

"I'm just keeping her temporarily," Annie said. "I can take her to a friend's house tomorrow afternoon. She's really very well mannered, Mr. Stigler."

"I don't care if she uses a napkin and can recite Emily Post," Stigler growled. "She's a four-legged animal—a pet—isn't she?"

"Yes, sir, but—"

"A clear violation of your lease, Miss Malloy."

"Mr. Stigler, I don't intend to keep her here after tomorrow. She's—"

"You have until 9:00 a.m. tomorrow morning to get her off the premises, Miss Malloy. I must be going soft in the head to let you keep her that long, but you've caused no trouble until now. If the dog's not gone by nine in the morning, however, I'll have to ask you to move."

"But I have to go to work in the morning."

"Then you can take her to work with you. 9:00 a.m., Miss Malloy. Not a minute later. And keep her quiet until then, or you'll have to get rid of her tonight." Stigler turned on his heel and stalked off.

"Old coot," Annie muttered as she shut the door. She let Callie out of the bathroom and took her into the bedroom. She coaxed Callie onto the foot of the bed and then settled back with a book. Callie squirmed and fidgeted and finally jumped off the bed to resume her pacing. She kept it up until Annie laid her book aside and turned out the light.

She didn't get much sleep. Callie roamed the apartment all night, whining every now and then and scratching at the front door. Once, after a particularly loud whine, a resident of the upstairs apartment banged something against the floor over Annie's bedroom.

Annie got up early and made scrambled eggs for herself and Callie, a farewell meal of sorts. The remains of the meat she'd fed Callie the evening before were still in her bowl, and she didn't eat all of her eggs, either. She's been cooped up for too long, Annie decided, first in the kennel and, during the last few days, in the small apartment. The cramped quarters must be making her fidgety.

There was only one solution to Annie's problem. As soon as her office opened at eight-thirty, she called to say she'd been unavoidably detained but hoped to make it to work by noon. Then she snapped on Callie's leash and took her out to the car.

If she'd known how to reach Sam, she'd have called to say she was taking Callie out to his place sooner than she'd planned. But she had no idea where Sam

was staying. She hoped to locate the neighbor Sam
mentioned and ask him to keep an eye on Callie until
Sam returned. If she couldn't find the neighbor, she
wasn't sure she could just drop Callie in Sam's yard
and drive away. She might have to call the office again
and say she wouldn't make it in at all.

Although she hadn't driven in the direction of
Sam's place for fifteen months, she found the gravel
country road without difficulty. The fields strewn with
yellow wildflowers looked all too familiar, bringing an
ache of nostalgia to Annie's throat. It was just as well,
she told herself, that she wasn't going to see Sam.

The only noticeable change since her last visit was
the new low-rise stone ranch house on Sam's property. She stopped in front of the double garage and put
Callie on the leash again. A space, about an acre in
size, had been fenced behind the house. The fence was
chain-link and almost as tall as Annie's head. The only
way a dog could possibly escape would be to dig out,
and basset hounds weren't good diggers. They were
handicapped by their short legs and the awkward angle of their front paws. Besides, there was no reason
for Callie to want to get out. The yard was big enough
for her to run to her heart's content, and there was a
back door opening into the garage if she wanted to go
inside.

Annie left her in the yard and fastened the gate. "I'll
be back in a little while," she promised. "I have to
find Sam's neighbor." Callie was busy sniffing the
perimeter of the yard when Annie left her.

Annie backed out of the drive and continued down
the road. She'd already checked the names on the
mailboxes in the other direction. A few hundred yards

beyond Sam's house, on the opposite side of the road, stood a black mailbox with Preston printed in white letters across its side. Annie turned down the narrow lane that led to a small, ramshackle frame house.

A shaggy, black mongrel slunk out from under the porch and barked as Annie got out of the car. She was afraid to go any closer. "Hello!" she called. "Is anybody home?"

A man in a worn blue work shirt and striped bib overalls came out of the house. "Shut up, Bud," he ordered, and the barking subsided. The man looked as though he spent most of his time out of doors. Annie judged him to be about fifty, but his skin was dark and leathery from the sun and wind. He hooked his thumbs on either side of his overalls bib and rocked back on his heels. "Howdy."

"Mr. Preston?"

"Yes'm. What can I do for you, ma'am?"

Annie eyed the dog who was eyeing her back. "Is it all right if I come up on the porch? Your dog doesn't seem to like me. What's his name again?"

Preston grinned. "That's Bud—short for Budweiser. He's partial to beer, but Budweiser's his favorite. Come on up. He ain't gonna bite you."

Annie walked cautiously past the dog, who sniffed her hand. Apparently satisfied that she was harmless, he bounded ahead of her up the porch steps and stood beside his master, wagging his tail when Preston placed a hand on top of the dog's head.

He's good with dogs, Annie thought, and immediately felt better about leaving Callie. She introduced herself and caught a whiff of beer on Preston's breath when they shook hands. At nine-thirty in the morning? Old Bud wasn't the only one who was partial to the suds, she thought dryly.

She told him about her joint inheritance with Sam, which Preston seemed to find hilarious. He slapped his leg and laughed until tears rolled out of the corners of his eyes. "Sam went all the way to California for a dog?" he asked as soon as he caught his breath. "I'll bet he was fit to be tied. Probably ranted and raved about all the work he could have been doing instead. Sam's a mite serious, he is. Probably couldn't see the joke in inheriting a dog."

"You're right, he couldn't." Annie didn't have time to explain that Callie was unique. "Mr. Preston, I just penned Callie—that's the basset hound—in Sam's yard. I have to get to work and I can't leave her in my apartment any longer. I was wondering if you'd be able to keep an eye on her until Sam gets home this evening. He should be here about seven-thirty."

"Why, sure. I'll check on her now and then. Thought I'd wet a fish hook in my bass pond this afternoon, but other than that I ain't got nothing to do all day."

"The back door to the garage is open, so Callie can go inside if she wants to. She'll need water, though. Do you have a pan I could borrow?"

"I'll give her some water. Something to eat, too. You go on to work, ma'am. The dog will be okay. I'll amble on over there right now and get acquainted."

"Thank you, Mr. Preston," Annie said with relief. "I've been so worried about leaving her in a strange place all day. You don't know how much I appreciate this."

Preston brushed aside her gratitude with a wave of his hand. "Don't mention it. And call me Jude."

Annie grinned. "If you'll call me Annie." She took a business card out of her purse and handed it to him. "You can reach me at that number, if you need to."

Preston tucked the card into his overalls pocket. "Don't you worry, now. Old Bud and me'll handle things here. Never met a dog who didn't take to me."

Her anxiety considerably eased, Annie drove away. She'd check on Callie tonight after Sam got home, just to confirm what she already knew. Sam's fence was basset-proof, and Jude Preston would keep an eye on Callie. What could go wrong?

Four

——

Annie started phoning Sam's house at seven-thirty that evening. At nine, when she still hadn't reached Sam, she looked up Jude Preston's number.

After identifying herself, Annie said, "Sam's not answering his phone. Have you seen him?"

"No, ma'am. Reckon his plane is late. You don't have to worry about Callie, though. She's settled down real good. I think she likes her new home."

Annie felt better when she hung up. She'd try Sam again in the morning.

The ringing of the telephone woke Annie from a deep sleep at 6:45 Thursday morning. "Just a minute," she mumbled as she struggled to a sitting position and tried to get her bearings. She reached for the phone beside the bed. "Hel—" She paused to clear her throat. "Hello?"

"Annie, it's Sam. Did I wake you?"

She sank back down on the pillow, her mind still sluggish with sleep. "It's okay. I should be up, anyway." Why was Sam calling at this ungodly hour? Then she remembered that she'd taken Callie to the house yesterday. "What's wrong?" she asked, alarmed. "You found Callie, didn't you? I left her there yesterday."

"She's right here in the kitchen with me," Sam assured her, "eating a hamburger. You're right, she won't eat dog food, and it's not just Chow Hound. I tried another brand."

"Oh, good," Annie sighed. "I thought—when you called so early... Why *are* you calling so early, Sam?"

"My flight was late. I didn't get home until two. I brought Callie in the house with me then, and she woke me at five-thirty, wanting to eat."

Interesting, but why was he calling before seven o'clock to tell her this? "I'm sorry, Sam. I'm sure she won't do that once she gets used to staying there."

"It's not that. I planned to work at home today, anyway. I'll catch a nap later."

Still perplexed, Annie said, "It was thoughtful of you to call and let me know Callie's all right."

"Actually, that's not the only reason I'm calling. I thought I better let you know we might have a small problem with Callie. We should talk it over."

Annie sat upright again, her growing anxiety throwing off the shreds of drowsiness left by the night's sleep. "Callie's not sick, is she?"

"No. She's full of vim and vinegar."

"Then what's the problem?"

"It's sort of involved, but nothing to worry about. I don't want to get into it now. It's something we should discuss face-to-face. Can you come out here this evening?"

"Sam—"

"Seven would be fine."

If it was nothing to worry about, why was he being so evasive? She felt irritated, but she knew that if Sam had made up his mind not to tell her now, he wouldn't. She remembered how defensive he could get when someone tried to pry something out of him that he didn't want to reveal. His stubborn refusal to share all his thoughts and feelings with her used to drive her crazy.

Annie stifled her impatience. "All right. I'll see you at seven."

Annie headed for Sam's house directly from the office. She'd worked overtime trying to finish collection calls on accounts that were at least three months in arrears. She'd reached all but two of the delinquents and had been assured by one and all that the check was in the mail or soon would be. Annie had heard that before and didn't put much stock in it. She wasn't tough enough, she decided. She was going to have to turn over some of the accounts to a real collection agency.

At Sam's, Callie went into a spasm of excitement as soon as she saw Annie. Annie laughed and embraced the dog. "Did you miss me, Callie?" After a few moments Callie calmed down enough for Annie to turn her attention to Sam, who was leaning against the wall of the foyer watching Annie and the dog with amusement.

He wore low-riding jeans and a striped polo shirt. He looked marvelous, though Annie was sure he had given no thought to his attire. Sam had never been interested in clothes. Annie's heartbeat speeded up.

"I like your house," she said. She scanned the wide, flagstone-floored foyer, then walked into the large living area that opened off the foyer at the back of the house. With its cedar-beamed cathedral ceiling, the room was open and inviting. A massive flagstone fireplace at one end of the room drew her attention. Around it was a grouping of blue-and-tan striped camel-back couch and several comfortable-looking armchairs in navy, wine and creamy beige. The back wall of the room was almost entirely glass and French doors leading to a huge redwood deck completed the effect.

Sam followed her, watching the quick, easy grace with which she walked. She wore a yellow dress that fit her narrow waist snugly, the full, gathered skirt swirling around her slender legs as she moved. She looked wonderful. Sam recalled the many times he'd pictured her here, the thousand shattering moments when he'd dreamed she looked exactly as she did now before he'd been able to push the image away. "Would you like to see the rest?"

"Oh, yes."

With Callie at their heels, Sam led the way down a wide hallway to the master suite: bedroom, sitting room and bath complete with twin marble washbasins, an oversize whirlpool tub and a separate shower stall.

"Lovely," Annie murmured. Her throat tightened as a bittersweet memory swept over her, a memory of leafing through decorating magazines with Sam to choose that very taupe-colored tub and the big wine and taupe floor tiles on which she stood.

Sam echoed her thoughts. "We worked out the plan for this bath together," Sam said.

"I remember."

The admission was a bit unsteady. The two softly spoken words seemed to whisper along Sam's skin.

Annie took a deep breath and turned around, almost colliding with Sam's chest. She stepped back hurriedly. "Excuse me.... Uh, what's next? The kitchen?" She wanted to get out of the master suite; it seemed to beckon her to intimacy everywhere she looked.

It took every ounce of Sam's determination not to reach for her. His mouth hungered for the taste of her skin. "The kitchen," he said hoarsely. He strode from the bathroom and quickly crossed the cream-colored carpet of the bedroom and sitting room. "The kitchen and breakfast room are the only other rooms I've finished," he added as soon as he could trust his voice again. "The dining room will be on the other side of the living room, the other bedrooms beyond that. I don't even have the wallboard up in there yet."

They walked into a big country kitchen with maple cabinets, almond-colored appliances, and rose-tinted Mexican tile on the floor. Annie spun around on her spike heels. "You did all of this yourself?"

"Except for laying the tile and building the cabinets. I didn't think my carpentry skills were up to that, so I contracted those jobs out."

She smiled at him. "It's perfect, Sam."

It was the smile that broke the back of his resolve. Up until then she'd seemed cool, controlled, but when she smiled at him, he saw the longing for things lost in her eyes. He didn't stop to ask himself if it was the house that so affected her, or himself.

Without taking his eyes from hers, he crossed the room and drew her hands into his. "We planned it down to the last detail."

"Yes, I know."

Sam gathered her into his arms. Strangely he felt as though he were standing back, watching himself embrace Annie and knowing he was a fool to do it. "We sat under that cottonwood tree at the back of the property and drew the plans for the kitchen," he murmured in her ear. "We brought a picnic lunch— chicken and potato salad and wine. Do you remember?"

Afterward they had made love, drowsy with the wine and the sunny autumn afternoon. Annie swallowed convulsively. "No. I—I guess it's been too long."

"Then why are you trembling?" His lips grazed her temple.

Annie felt her bones melting, her muscles weakening. "I—I'm not trembling."

"Liar." Beneath his thumb, he could feel the erratic flutter of her heartbeat at the side of her neck. "You still want me."

His breath feathered her forehead intimately. The need to lift her face and seek his mouth with hers was so strong that she almost groaned. "It's not like it was, not anymore."

He cupped her face in his hands and looked down at her with darkened eyes. "How is it, then, Annie?" he muttered. "Why is your heart beating as fast as if you'd run miles? Why are you here?"

She stiffened. "You asked me to come. You said we needed to talk about Callie." Her breathing was shallow and fast. Her eyes were nearly black. "Was that just a ruse to get me here?"

For an instant his fingers tightened on either side of her head and she could see the anger in his eyes. Then he released her so abruptly she almost lost her balance. He turned his back, but she knew he was trying to get control of his emotions. It gave her a chance to clutch the edge of the counter and steady herself. She hardly noticed Callie planted at her feet and making little whimpering sounds.

When he spoke, it was with rigid composure. "Callie is in heat."

"Heat?" Annie echoed, blank for the space of a few seconds. "Oh." Of course. That explained Callie's sudden restlessness. "You mean she can get pregnant? No wonder she's been acting so fidgety. I thought she was sick."

"Not unless you can call the sex drive a sickness," Sam said grimly. It wasn't a bad description, he added to himself.

"So." She drew her breath in sharply, as if waking from a dream in which she was falling, falling endlessly. "That isn't such a big problem, is it? We just have to be sure she's not with any male dogs for a while. You might have to keep her in the house when you're not able to watch her."

He turned around and looked at her for a long moment. "When I got home at 2:00 a.m. this morning, Jude Preston's dog was in the yard with Callie. He must've jumped the fence. I put him out and brought Callie inside, but he'd probably been here for some time."

"Bud?" Annie croaked, appalled at the thought of what puppies sired by that black mongrel would look like. Jude Preston had *promised* to keep an eye on Callie. Annie was suddenly so angry at Sam's neighbor she wanted to scream in frustration.

"I thought we should discuss it, in case... We may have lucked out. Depends on how long she's been in season. You were with her until yesterday morning. How—"

Before Sam could finish his inquiry as to how long Callie had been "fidgety," there was a knock at the door. Sam muttered an impatient oath and went to answer it.

Annie knelt beside Callie, who whined and licked her chin. "Poor baby," she soothed, stroking Callie's sleek coat. Sam was probably just trying to make her feel better by saying they might have lucked out. Bud had been in the yard with Callie, undoubtedly for hours. Of course Callie was pregnant!

Sam came back into the kitchen and pulled out a bottom drawer. "It's Jude. He wants to borrow a pipe wrench."

Annie looked up and saw Jude Preston standing in the kitchen doorway, grinning devilishly as if he'd caught Sam and Annie in a compromising position. "Howdy, ma'am." He swayed a little and steadied himself by gripping the doorjamb. How could he stand there, silly drunk, as if his stupid dog hadn't . . . Annie saw red.

She shot to her feet. "Do you know what your— drunken dog has done?" she sputtered.

Preston kept grinning. "Huh?"

"Bud," Annie said, in case he was too drunk to remember his dog's name. "Bud has impregnated California!"

Preston blinked at her and actually giggled. Then he drawled with infinite patience, "Ma'am, that ain't possible. Bud ain't never been any farther west than the county line."

Annie heard Sam behind her, choking on a laugh. She didn't think Preston was the least bit amusing! "California is the basset hound," she snapped.

"Oh, Callie." Preston shrugged off the news. "Bud can't help himself, ma'am. It's his nature."

Annie felt a headache coming on. As she pressed her index fingers to her temples, Sam got control of himself and hurried Preston out of the house. "Here's the wrench, Jude. Keep it as long as you need it."

"I reckon she's mad at me," Preston mumbled as they reached the front porch.

"Don't worry about it," Sam said. "She'll get over it." He stood on the porch for a few minutes after Preston was gone, waiting until he could keep a straight face before rejoining Annie.

The sight of Bud's owner had brought the passionate blaze to her eyes that he remembered so well. Nothing made Annie more furious than the thought of harm coming to someone she loved—and she adored Callie. So she had planted her hands on her hips and attacked Preston with all the vigor of a lioness protecting her cub.

Since Sam was half-convinced they had nothing to worry about—and even if they had, it wasn't the end of the world—he could see the humor in Annie's outrage. It had always surprised him how quickly Annie's temper could flare, and then how soon the storm would be over. Sam chuckled softly, remembering how Annie used to make him laugh. He realized it had been a long, long time since he'd found much to laugh about.

When Sam returned to the kitchen, Annie's outrage hadn't fully run its course. "I'm glad you find Callie's predicament amusing," she greeted him.

Sam couldn't suppress another chuckle. "You were pretty hard on Jude."

"*I* was hard on *him*! He was supposed to take care of Callie."

"I'm sure he checked on her several times before he went to bed. He didn't know Bud was in my yard until this morning when I told him."

"It's hard to believe that Bud could jump high enough to clear your fence."

"Jude claims he can jump a seven-foot fence when he's on the trail of a rabbit." His eyes smiled. "Obviously, Callie has the same effect on him."

"Wonderful. So what are we going to do?"

"Don't borrow trouble, Annie. I read the write-up in my encyclopedia on dog breeding. A dog's heat cycle lasts about three weeks, but she usually can't be bred during the first seven days. I didn't think that Callie was especially restless when we got to your apartment Saturday night. She seemed eager to go outside, but she'd been penned up for a long time. How did she act Sunday?"

"She was fine," Annie said. "In fact, she seemed perfectly content until Tuesday evening."

"I've never been around dogs, but if she didn't come in season until Tuesday, we're probably safe."

"We can't simply wait and see," Annie said, wary of accepting the assurance Sam was offering. "If she's pregnant, she'll need vitamins and special care. And we'll need to find homes for the puppies."

"We'd better hope that isn't the case," Sam said. A note of gravity had crept into his voice.

"Why?"

"The copies of those contracts came from Barnes while I was in Houston. Callie is scheduled to make another commercial in six weeks. Dogs carry their young about sixty days. If Callie is bred, she'll look very pregnant in six weeks' time. We can't deliver her in that condition for taping."

"But what can we do about it?"

"That's spelled out in the contract, too. After the six-week due date, we'll pay a fee for every day that Callie isn't available for taping. It could cost us a great deal of money."

"Oh, dear." Annie ran both hands through her hair in frustration. "I can't stand not knowing. We have to take her to a vet."

"I'd already reached that conclusion. That's what I wanted to discuss with you. I know a vet I can call. I think he'll work Callie in tomorrow if I ask him. If Callie's not bred, we can stop worrying about it. If she is, we'll have some time to come up with the money. In any event, we have to think about getting her spayed, Annie. There's no good reason for us to go through this every six months."

"You're right," Annie said fervently. "Not with Bud living across the road."

His eyes met hers and a hint of a smile played across his mouth. "Good. I'll go call the vet. While I'm doing that, would you mind checking our dinner in the smoker on the deck?"

"Dinner? But I didn't plan—"

"There's plenty for two," Sam said, heading for the telephone in his bedroom.

Not knowing what else to do, Annie wandered out to the deck. Only then did she see the small table at one end of the deck. It was covered with a white cloth and plates and silverware for two. There was even a bouquet of flowers in the center of the table. In the quickly falling dusk, Annie couldn't tell what kind of flowers they were until she walked to the table.

Red roses. Annie had always loved red roses. She bent and buried her face in the velvet petals, thinking of how cleverly Sam had planned this. She now realized that they could have easily discussed Callie's problem over the telephone. It almost seemed like Sam was trying to please her—as though he were courting her again.

But why? A gust of wind caught the corner of the tablecloth, and Annie smoothed it into place again. The sky had been overcast when she'd left work. Now the wind had brought the faint scent of approaching rain.

What was behind Sam's little dinner? Annie shivered, afraid that she knew very well what Sam was up to. He still hadn't forgiven her for walking out on him.

What if this was Sam's way of getting revenge? What if he meant to seduce her, force her to face her feelings for him, and then . . .

"Annie?"

Annie jumped at the sound of Sam's voice. "Over here."

He peered at her curiously, trying to discern her expression in the dim twilight. She sounded odd. But she was still here; he wouldn't have been surprised if she'd left while he was on the telephone—disappointed but not surprised. "Did you check the brisket?"

"Not yet."

"Never mind. I'll do it. Why don't you get the wine from the refrigerator?" He went to a black charcoal smoker set at the edge of the deck. Snagging a long fork from a hook at the side of the smoker, he lifted the lid.

He heard her stir, cross the deck and go inside. The brisket was done to perfection. Using two forks, he lifted it onto a platter. At least she was staying for dinner, he thought, but he cautioned himself not to imagine it meant anything more than that.

To Sam, it meant he was one step closer to proving to himself that she still had feelings for him—and believing that whatever *he* still felt for her could be alleviated by making love to her one last time. She was a human being, too, dammit, a flesh and blood woman, and he knew several that he could have for the asking. What was it about Annie that he found so irresistible? She was volatile, passionate; when Annie's heart was engaged, she held back nothing. Maybe it was this that had drawn him. He had often wondered how someone learned to be so incautious, so free.

Lord, he wanted her still. The need rose like a demon through layers of pride, arousing him even as he thought about satisfying that need. There was a time when she'd wanted him just as much, had been unable to get enough of him. But her appetite hadn't stopped with the physical. She had wanted to know all his secrets—the doubts, the guilt, the resentment, the pain. These were things he'd never shared with anyone, and he didn't think he ever could. He had tried to explain that to Annie, but how could someone so open and giving understand?

His refusal had hurt her, though he hadn't meant it to. She had changed, becoming more guarded. Finally she had left him. In the midst of his desolation, he'd been fiercely glad he hadn't been able to give what she'd asked. He had kept one small corner of himself, and it was because of that hard, self-protective core that he was able to survive after Annie was gone.

The branches of an elm tree near the deck swayed with a sudden gust of cool wind. Sam lifted his head and sniffed rain. It would storm later tonight, but not until after he and Annie had eaten dinner.

There had been a few other women in the past fifteen months. To his shame, every one of them had reminded him of Annie in some small way—dark curly hair, big brown eyes, a certain way of moving. Now Annie was back in his life, however tentatively. He was determined to have her again, and this time he knew her vulnerabilities. This time when it was over, he would be the one who walked away.

* * *

Dinner was delicious. Barbecued brisket, spinach salad, crisply steamed cauliflower and carrots in a light, tangy cheese sauce and thick slabs of crunchy toast, sweet with melted butter. Sam was a better cook than she was, Annie reflected, and he hadn't even known how to cook when he lived in the apartment. Annie was not surprised by Sam's recently acquired skill, however. Sam was so competent it was almost scary. Wasn't he building a house with his own hands in his "spare time"?

Sam was adept at many things, Annie thought ruefully. Look how easily he had maneuvered her into staying. In her own defense, she had been tired and hungry. But that wasn't the reason she'd stayed. She'd stayed because she'd finally stopped lying to herself.

In the kitchen earlier, he would have kissed her if Jude Preston hadn't appeared, and Annie had wanted him to kiss her more than she'd ever wanted anything. Ever since he'd kissed her Saturday night in her apartment, she had hoped it would happen again; tonight she had simply admitted it to herself.

The wind was stronger than when they'd started eating, and cooler. Annie pulled the sweater Sam had lent her closer together in front. Callie had been shut in the house while they ate for fear she would somehow get out of the yard, and Annie smiled when she saw the dog on the other side of the glass partition. Callie's nose was pressed against the pane and her big eyes were eloquent with her desire to be with them.

Freddy must have spent most of his time with her, talked to her like a person, pampered her. Given his lack of relationships with people, his attachment to the dog must have been the center of his life. As far as Annie knew, Freddy had never had a serious involvement with a woman. And except for Sam, whom he hadn't seen again after leaving Oklahoma, Annie suspected Freddy had made no other close friends. She also knew that if Freddy had lived, both she and Sam would have heard from him eventually. He'd probably been waiting until he was sure of Callie's continuing success. He'd wanted to prove to her and Sam that he wasn't a failure.

Still, more than anyone she knew—even more than Sam—Freddy had not seemed to need other people. It was a trait Annie could never understand, because at times she simply had to have someone to talk to, someone to laugh with, someone to touch. During the last fifteen months, she had tried to cut away that part of herself, to make her work satisfy all her needs, but the empty place left in her life by Sam's absence still remained.

"Annie, would you like more wine?"

She'd almost forgotten where she was. "Yes, please." The soft moan of the tree branches swaying in the wind had a hypnotic effect. Annie was feeling lazy, drowsily content and reluctant to move.

Sam refilled her glass. "You were far away for a few minutes. What were you thinking about?"

She smiled. "Freddy."

"He was a strange little guy," Sam mused, "but I always liked him."

"I felt sorry for him because he was such a drifter, so detached from everything around him. But I suppose he was happy enough."

"Or wanted people to think he was."

A raindrop plopped on the arm of Annie's chair. "It's going to rain," she said, sad that they would have to go inside and the spell of contentment would be broken. She rose. "We'd better take the dishes in."

They did so, working quickly and silently together. Sam gave Callie the scraps of food left on their plates, and Annie loaded the dishwasher and added powdered detergent. Rain began to fall gently on the roof.

When there were no more dishes to put into the dishwasher, Annie set the dial and turned to find Sam watching her. "The road out front turns to mush when it rains," he said matter-of-factly.

Annie knew in that moment what was going to happen, and she accepted it as inevitable. She felt relieved that the decision had been made. Yet she couldn't meet Sam's eyes.

Sam covered the few steps separating them, cupped her head in his hands and tilted it. She stared up at him, all at once beset by nervousness and doubts. What if Sam was disappointed in her, after all? But neither of them could turn back now. Everything that had transpired this evening had, in some incomprehensible way, been leading up to this point.

Sam didn't move for a long moment as he studied her face. Her hair was tangled, her skin pale in the soft kitchen light, and he could see her reflection in the black windowpane behind her. Her eyes were dark and a bit dazed by a mingling of misgiving and desire. As he watched, she sighed and closed her eyes as though what she saw in his was too real, too much truth to be taken in all at once. Then she moistened her lips with the tip of her tongue, an action that made Sam suck in his breath.

He lowered his head and traced her features gently with his mouth—her temple, a dark, curving brow, the hollow of her cheek, the angle of her jaw just below her ear—nibbling, lingering, learning the taste of her again.

She murmured and turned her head so that his lips brushed her searching mouth with soft, exquisite care. His thumb stroked the sensitive skin just below her jawline, and the tip of his tongue lightly traced her bottom lip. Annie shuddered and her hands went around his neck, clinging.

He nuzzled into the side of her neck, nibbling and heating her skin with his breath. When he lifted his head, her mouth was waiting, wet and greedy. Passion shook them. A clap of thunder rocked the house, and Annie gripped his shoulders reflexively.

"Take...me...to...your...bed..." she whispered breathlessly, getting the words out one at a time between kisses that became progressively deeper and more desperate. "I want you, Sam."

Hardly breaking the kiss, Sam scooped her into his arms and carried her to the bedroom. Gently he lowered her to the bed and stood looking down at her. The bedroom lay in shadow, but a jagged flash of lightning illuminated Sam's face for an instant. He looked like a statue hewn of stone, except for the eyes that were chaotic with passion. Annie reached up to touch him, and he grasped her hand, pressing his warm mouth into the palm.

Then he bent over her and, with unsteady fingers, began to undo the buttons of her dress. Seized by the fire of need, Annie tried to unbutton his shirt at the same time. They were clumsy in their desperate eagerness. Finally, Sam freed her last button and pulled the dress over her head. When he took off her clinging silk slip, Annie heard the fabric rip, but she was past caring about anything except the need to feel Sam's hard, naked body pressing against hers.

"I tore your slip," he murmured. "I'm sorry." He freed her of her panties and panty hose.

"It doesn't matter." She watched him strip off his shirt and peel down his jeans. "Come here."

He removed the remnants of his clothing and the mattress gave under his weight. "You're more beautiful than ever," he whispered.

As he lowered his full length over her, she wound her arms around his neck. Anticipation trembled through her, and she saw his shadowed face above her. She felt dazed in the brief moment before his mouth crushed hers.

Thunder cracked and rain came down in a torrent. "I need you," Annie murmured. "Oh, Sam, I need you so much."

"I want it to last," he muttered, and deliberately changed the kiss from desperate to languorous. For a little while Annie was able to forget the heavy tension in the pit of her stomach as she lost herself in the pleasure of the kiss. His mouth tasted of wine, his lips were so soft and moist. His tongue made a languid exploration of her mouth.

Annie moved against him sensuously, invitingly, while her hands skimmed the smooth, warm skin of his back and came to rest on his lean flanks.

She was so soft and sweet. The touch of her body, her hands, excited him. But he wanted to savor her, to pleasure her endlessly. His hand stroked down her side, lingering on the soft cushion of her breast, the narrow curve of her waist, the gentle rounding of her hip. Then he raised up on his hands and lowered his head until his mouth found the peak of her breast.

"Oh, Sam...." Annie arched against him, her body shuddering with the hunger ripping through her. She wanted him to hurry, wanted him to forget tenderness and take her with a hard, primitive passion. Her hand slid between their bodies, seeking him.

The touch of her hand drove Sam wild. She was all fire and need beneath him, moving and arching as her breath came in soft, incoherent moans. He fought to retain his self-control, but it was slipping, shredding fast. His breathing was ragged as he rose up on his knees and, grasping her hips, lifted her.

Her skin was damp and quivering. Her hands reached out for him, clutching his shoulders, her fingers digging into his flesh. He heard a roaring and didn't know if it was the thunder outside or the pounding of his own blood in his head. He entered her with one long, sure thrust and the world exploded.

He thought he heard Annie cry his name. Then she wrapped herself around him and moved with him. His open mouth took hers and he tasted the salt of her tears. The storm raged, inside as well as outside, and as he plunged into its eye, his heart cried out, *My Annie.... Mine!*

Five

His hand lay on her hip. Her head rested on the curve of his shoulder and her hand was spread on his chest. She could feel the slow, dull thud of his heart. Annie sighed with contentment. She felt too drowsy and serene to be sorry for what had happened. Perhaps she would regret it later, but not now, not while she was nestled against Sam's warm body with his arm around her and his hand idly stroking light circles on her hip.

Rain splattered steadily against the windows and Annie wondered if the road was passable, but she'd deal with that thought later. A deep rumble of thunder shook the house, making her shiver and snuggle closer to Sam.

"You're cold." He raised himself up and felt for the edge of the sheet tangled between them. After pulling the sheet over both of them, he asked, "That better?'' and drew her to him again. Annie resettled her head on his shoulder and extended her arm across his chest.

''Umm, much.''

He kissed her brow softly and they were silent for a few moments, suspended in the golden afterglow of their lovemaking, listening to the rain on the roof.

''Annie,'' Sam murmured finally. ''What are you thinking?''

She laughed and hugged his waist. ''That's my line, Sam.''

He laughed then, too, remembering how she used to say that she wanted to know everything about him, *everything*. ''I forgot myself for a minute there,'' he said, smiling. ''You've addled me, Annie.''

''Do you really want to know what I was thinking?'' Annie asked.

''Yeah.''

''I was thinking that I owe my parents a letter.'' He took a playful swat at her bottom, and she laughed. ''Sorry, Sam, but you asked.'' The truth was, she'd been wondering if she should break the news to her parents about the joint inheritance, and whether it would be better not to mention that Sam was the other heir. If they knew, they'd only worry about her. Though she'd tried to hide it, she'd sensed they suspected how much she had suffered when she and Sam had broken up.

''How are they?''

''Couldn't be better. They recently bought a condo in Key Largo. Mom's helping organize craft shows, and Dad has plenty of fishing and golfing buddies. They want me to spend my vacation with them.''

"Will you?"

"I haven't decided yet. I *am* dying to see them, but I may just fly down for a weekend. The only problem is that Mom already had two weeks' worth of activities planned for us."

"You and your mother have a great relationship. I always envied that a little." In fact, early in their relationship, Sam had been jealous of Annie's love for her parents. He hadn't known he was capable of such petty feelings, and he'd been ashamed of them. Annie had never known, and later, when he felt more secure in the relationship, he'd conquered the jealousy.

Annie lifted herself on one elbow and looked down at him. She couldn't see his expression in the darkness. She traced the angle of his cheek with one finger. "You envied what I have with my mother? Is that because you didn't have that kind of relationship with your mother?"

"I hardly knew her."

His tone was tense suddenly, and Annie felt a muscle in his jaw tighten beneath her hand. "I'm sorry, Sam. She's dead, isn't she?"

He pulled her down beside him, wrapped his arms around her and buried his face in her hair. "I don't know." The words were muffled.

"Oh, Sam—"

"I don't want to talk about it, Annie."

I don't want to talk about it. How many times had she heard those words when they were together? Why wouldn't he talk about his parents, his childhood?

And why did she let his refusal frustrate her so? In the silence that followed Sam's words, Annie wondered, as she had when they were together, if Sam's self-sufficiency and unwillingness to open up to people was some kind of elaborate defense constructed when he was a little boy because, in some way, his parents had let him down. Questions with no answers, she reflected and tried to smother her frustration.

She sighed. "If you don't want to talk about it, then God knows you won't." She sat up. "Where's my bra?"

His hand clasped her shoulder. "I didn't mean to be short with you, Annie." He was doing it again, he realized. Why did he always drive Annie away when all he wanted to do was hold her, cherish her? He'd meant to sound more apologetic, but he couldn't find the right words. He'd always had trouble admitting weakness. "Don't go."

"Oh, Sam, what's the use?"

"Don't say that," he said fiercely, and drew her back into his arms.

Near tears, Annie threw her arms around him and buried her face against his throat. I love him, she thought, I never stopped loving him. Somehow, simply forming the words in her mind released some of her anguish.

"I've missed you," Sam said hoarsely. "God, how I've missed you. I wish I could be what you want." He would have said anything in that moment to keep her there even a little while longer.

She lifted her head and settled her body firmly on top of his. She rained kisses on his face. "Shh," she whispered. "Right now I just want you to make love to me. Is it too soon?"

For an answer, he rolled her over until he loomed above her. He lowered his mouth to hers, and as his tongue entered her mouth, she felt the hardening of his body against her stomach.

The rain had slackened to a soft drizzle, but neither of them noticed. The bedroom was a warm, quiet, enchanted place where the world could not intrude. Moist flesh slid easily against moist flesh, hands caressed secret places, hungry mouths sought remembered textures and tastes.

The only sounds were the gentle whisper of rain on the window and soft sighs building slowly in intensity. This time they were able to hold the fire back longer, to draw out the pleasure while they took their fill of each other.

Floating on a sea of lovely sensations, Annie stretched languidly beneath him, wanting every inch of her damp flesh to feel the weight of him. While his hungry mouth crushed hers, his hands roamed over her, searching, stroking, caressing. She wanted to go on feeling like this forever.

But then his fingers found the moist core of her womanhood and shot fire through her. Her control snapped. She moved against him, arching desperately, wanting more. She was riding the crest of a wave, going higher and higher. Thrashing, she cried out his name.

Sam's blood roared in his ears. Hearing her call out for him broke the last threads of his control. Groaning, he slid his hands up her body. She reached for him greedily and drew him inside of her. There was nothing then but wave upon wave of feeling.

Later they lay tangled in each other's arms, spent. "Thank you, Annie," Sam murmured, shifting so that her body molded perfectly to his.

"My pleasure."

"It's stopped raining."

"Mmm."

They were silent for long moments. Annie was drifting toward sleep when Sam spoke again.

"My mother walked out on me and my father." His tone was sad, desolate. "After that, my father—well, he was never the same again."

Annie opened her eyes, afraid to move, almost afraid to breathe. She knew what it had cost Sam to say even that much. She couldn't speak, so she turned her head and pressed her mouth against his neck. His arms tightened around her.

"The road isn't as bad as I made it sound," he whispered. "I didn't want you to leave. Will you stay the night?"

She tilted her head back and looked up at him. She could barely see the outline of his face in the darkness. "Yes, if you want me to."

"I want you more than anything, Annie..." he said on a long sigh before they both slept.

Callie woke them a while later, jumping on the bed and flopping full-length across their legs.

"What's going on?" Sam mumbled, thrashing and pushing Callie to the foot of the bed.

Annie yawned and snuggled into Sam's warm side. "She's used to sleeping on a bed. I let her do it when she stayed with me."

Sam sat up while Annie turned on her side and drew her knees up, ready to drift back to sleep. Sam shoved

Callie off the side of the bed. "She'll just have to get used to the floor. There isn't room in this bed for three." He lay back down and curved his body to fit Annie's back, resting a hand on her hip.

Callie made her displeasure known by letting out a heart-rending howl. Then she stood at Sam's side of the bed and barked.

"Quiet, Callie!" Sam growled. Callie made a snuffling sound full of self-pity and plodded out of the room. "She's pining for old Bud," Sam murmured against Annie's hair.

Annie giggled. "Poor Callie has atrocious taste in men."

Sam's hand curved around Annie's breast, and within seconds he was breathing deeply and evenly. By that time Annie was wide-awake. She lay still, not wanting to disturb Sam, and stared into the darkness, thinking.

Had it been a mistake to spend the night with Sam? She guessed it really didn't matter that much, once she'd gotten into Sam's bed in the first place. If there had been a mistake, it was letting things get to that point. She wasn't naive enough to think that just because Sam had finally said two sentences about his parents, he'd changed in any basic way. People weren't transformed overnight; she didn't want to delude herself. She was very much afraid that her reasons for leaving Sam fifteen months ago were still warranted.

Sam wasn't asleep, only pretending to be. It felt so good to have Annie back in his bed. Sweet, impulsive, funny Annie. Why was it Annie, of all the women he'd known, who could get past his defenses to the soft center where long ago he'd buried his childhood pain and vulnerability?

Already he half regretted telling Annie about his parents. He knew that Annie was a sucker for a sob story. Had he been trying to make her feel sorry for him by telling her? He couldn't accept that about himself. God, no. The last thing he wanted from Annie was pity. In fact, he told himself as he drifted slowly toward sleep, he couldn't afford to want anything lasting from Annie. She had the power to hurt him too badly.

When he awoke, lemon-colored sunlight splashed lavishly over the bed and carpet, warming his skin. Sam closed his eyes again and stretched lazily. Remembering the pleasures of the previous night, he reached for Annie. His arm closed on nothingness.

His eyes flew open and he sat up, alarmed. Then he heard her talking to Callie in the kitchen. The tantalizing scent of sizzling bacon drifted to him and he hastily climbed out of bed, pulling on a T-shirt and jeans.

A few minutes later Sam entered the kitchen. Annie, looking unwittingly seductive in nothing but one of his long-tailed cotton shirts, stood at the range, turning bacon in a skillet. Callie sat at Annie's feet, watching her every move with total concentration.

Annie turned her head and saw him. After a split second of awkward silence, she smiled. In that wordless instant Annie and Sam admitted that the previous night had not appreciably changed anything. There were still too many things unsaid, too many issues unresolved. It hadn't been a simple one-night stand for old times' sake, but there were still things to work through before they could either move closer to each other or walk away without leaving the best part of themselves behind. Neither of them knew where to start.

"Good morning, sleepyhead," Annie said as the moment passed.

"You been up long?" Sam asked as he kissed the back of her neck.

"Hours. I watched the sun rise." She set the skillet off the burner and turned into his arms.

"Trouble sleeping?" His eyes searched her face as he caught her close.

"Callie woke me," Annie told him in a breathless whisper. "She wanted to go out and, of course, I had to watch her..."

"In case Bud has the place staked out," he finished for her. He kissed her lightly.

She leaned against him for a moment, returning the kiss. "I have to take the biscuits out of the oven," she sighed, pulling away. "Coffee's made."

He poured coffee into a mug and sipped it, lounging against the counter while Annie made gravy from the bacon drippings. "I've decided not to go to work today," she told him. "I want to be with Callie at the vet's. So if you need to go to the office, I've got things covered here."

"There's nothing at the office that can't wait another day. I'll go with you."

With a laugh, she studied him, her head cocked to one side. "Playing hooky two days in a row, Bennington? Are you sure you're feeling well?"

"I feel..." He took a sip of coffee, giving himself time to think. "Domestic, I guess."

"My word. Watch it or you'll be calling for a pipe and slippers."

He grinned. "I had something a bit more active in mind. Callie's not expected at the vet's until ten-thirty."

She shook her head in mock chagrin. "Domestic, huh? Try lascivious."

"That, too."

"After breakfast," she said, flushing prettily. "I'm about to faint from starvation."

Two hours later they arrived at the square, buff-brick veterinary clinic on the western edge of Oklahoma City and took Callie inside.

Dr. Moses was a burly, blond man who appeared to be in his late twenties. He looked like a college wrestler, but after observing his gentleness with an injured kitten and its near-hysterical mistress, Annie decided he didn't have the killer instinct needed to excel in the sport.

Once the kitten was tended to and returned to its considerably calmer owner, the vet turned his attention to Sam, who introduced him to Annie. Moses rubbed Callie's head, then let her sniff his hand and arm until she lost interest.

"So," Moses said, gesturing for Sam to lift Callie up on the examining table. "She's the first TV star I've ever had in here. The old hormones acting up, are they, girl?"

He gave Callie a thorough examination before filling out a medical form with Sam and Annie's help. At length he said, "She hasn't been bred. If you want to make sure she stays that way, you should keep her penned up for at least sixteen more days. Three weeks, just to be sure."

"We've decided to have her spayed," Annie said. "I wish we'd thought of it before this happened. Now I guess we'll have to wait."

"That's a common misconception," Moses said. "The fact is, we spay dogs who are in heat all the time, especially if they're in their first week, as Callie is."

"Really?" Annie looked at Sam.

"Yep. It's perfectly safe. I can do it this afternoon, in fact, and you can take her home tomorrow."

"Then why don't we let you go ahead," Sam said. "Get it over with."

Annie agreed. At noon, they left Callie in Dr. Moses's capable hands and found a restaurant. They sat at a small table covered with red-checked cloth. The scent of grilling beef and onions was strong and the speakers high up in two corners of the restaurant poured out a series of country songs, tales of honky tonks, wild women, and broken hearts. Their waitress was a loud-mouthed redhead who tipped the scales somewhere between two hundred and two-fifty. Her name badge read Sally.

At Sally's suggestion, they ordered steak sandwiches. Cupping her chin in one hand, Annie said, "Some ambience, Bennington. I'm impressed."

"Thought you would be." He gave her a devilish wink. "Now tell me I don't know how to show a woman a good time."

She smiled, twirling a straw in her glass of cola. "You have your moments." She drew on the straw. When she lifted her head, a drop of moisture quivered at the corner of her mouth. Sam promptly took care of that by leaning across the table and kissing it away.

Annie gazed at him provocatively from beneath half-lowered lashes. "Do you believe Freddy can see us now?"

"I'd like to think so. He'd be so damned smug about the way Callie has brought us together."

"In a manner of speaking."

Sam contemplated her for a long moment. "Yeah."

"When did you meet him?"

Sam took his elbows off the table so that the waitress could set plates laden with thick, juicy steak sandwiches in front of them. She popped her gum and jerked her straining dress down over her ample stomach. "You need any ketchup or steak sauce?"

"Not for me," Annie said.

"No, thanks, this is fine." Sam watched the waitress walk away, her fat buns bouncing. "Amazing," he commented, making Annie giggle.

"Seventh grade," Sam said, taking up the conversation where the waitress had interrupted it. "We had a class bully."

"Doesn't every class."

"Sure. It's obligatory. This one's name was Herbert, but he insisted that we call him Duke."

"Which you were more than happy to do."

He took a bite of his sandwich, meeting Annie's laughing eyes as he chewed and swallowed. "Naturally. Well, the first day of school Duke chose Freddy to be the brunt of his jokes. When the fun went out of that, he started beating up on Freddy every day after school. I was big for my age—got my growth spurt early—and I felt sorry for Freddy. We lived near each other, so I began walking home with him. The next time Duke picked a fight, Freddy and I beat the socks off him. Bloodied his nose and blackened one eye. God, it felt good."

Annie raised a teasing brow. "Not to Duke."

"Nope, but he steered clear of us after that. Freddy and I remained fast friends all the way through high school. I later moved to Norman to work and attend the university, but I was always sure to look him up when I was back in town. The last time I saw him was about two weeks before he left Oklahoma for good. He'd just moved out of your apartment and needed a place to stay, so I let him use my couch for a few days."

Annie's mouth twisted a bit sadly. "I would guess that Freddy slept on several couches around town at one time or another. He was out of work as often as not."

"Couldn't find his niche," Sam agreed.

"Until he got Callie." Annie sipped her drink. "I'm glad he had her in the last days of his life."

Sam watched her press a paper napkin to her mouth. "The last thing Freddy ever said to me was, 'You and Annie belong together, but you're both too damned stubborn to see it.'"

Annie moved her shoulders. "Stubbornness had nothing to do with it. It was . . . oh, irreconcilable differences, I guess."

Sam waited for her to go on, but she lifted her sandwich instead and took a bite, avoiding his gaze. Was she trying to tell him something more without saying the words? Maybe she had left him for the obvious reason that she didn't love him anymore. Maybe she was trying to say that things hadn't really changed that much, either.

So how had last night happened? How was it that he had nearly drowned in their mutual passion? *Don't be a jerk, Bennington,* he told himself. Sexually they were obviously very compatible, but that didn't mean she loved him.

Well, he'd take what he could get until he got his fill of her. If that ever happened, a small voice nagged. Abruptly he changed the subject and Annie seemed relieved. They were both careful to keep the conversation on a casual plane for the remainder of the meal.

They looked in on Callie after the surgery. She was still sedated and resting comfortably. "We'll give her a little something to help her sleep through the night," Dr. Moses told them. "You can pick her up any time before five tomorrow afternoon."

"I'll do it," Sam told Annie as they left the clinic.

"Sure you don't mind?" Annie asked, remembering her promise to take care of visits to the vet.

"I'm sure."

They got in Sam's car and headed for his house. "As soon as Callie feels better," Annie said, "we have to put her on a regular training schedule. We should be going through her tricks with her two or three times a week."

"Hmm," Sam murmured absently.

"I'll bet we could teach her other tricks, too. She's obviously quick. I can come out after work and do it."

"We'll work it out."

Sam seemed to have his mind on other things, so Annie let the subject drop.

"Annie," Sam ventured after a few moments of silence, "tomorrow's Saturday. Why don't you stay at my place again tonight?" He tried to make the question sound like a casual impulse, careful not to look at her as he said it.

Annie fought the desire to fling caution to the wind and accept Sam's invitation. She was still in love with him, God help her, but another night in his bed could only expose her to more hurt in the end. In the clear light of day, she was forced to acknowledge that Sam still didn't need her—or anyone—not really, not at the deep, meaningful level where she needed him.

"Not a good idea," she said finally.

"I think it's a terrific idea," he said quietly.

Annie thought of his spotless house. She'd left Sam's shirt, the one she'd worn that morning, hanging on a bedpost. She tried to remember if she'd left her towel on the bathroom floor after her shower that morning and feared that she had. She'd probably left the cap off the toothpaste, as well—a bad habit of hers. In only a few hours, then, she'd managed to clutter up Sam's orderly little world. She sighed inwardly, telling herself that she and Sam probably didn't have a chance of making it together, even if he did love her. They were destined to drive each other crazy.

"Terrific," she admitted at last, "but not wise. I'm going to have to go to the office for a few hours tomorrow and try to get caught up."

"I see," Sam said, not really believing that she needed to work on Saturday. "Do you do that often—work overtime?"

"Frequently."

He glanced at her thoughtfully. "You never used to be a workaholic."

She might have said she had learned to use work to keep her mind off other things—like Sam. "I must have caught it from you," she said lightly. But, she reflected, Sam seemed more relaxed about his work now than he had when they were together. In those days he wouldn't have taken time off to deliver a dog to the vet.

Her remark made Sam defensive, but he didn't want to argue with her. "Obviously we both need to learn to relax. Why don't you reconsider and stay over again." Almost as soon as the words were out, Sam regretted them. It sounded too much like begging.

Annie sighed. "Sam, we both need space and time to think. So I'll just pick up my car at your place and go on home."

She was wrong, Sam thought. What he needed at that moment was to lose himself in Annie so that he wouldn't have to think. But he didn't say that. He still had some pride left.

Six

———

Annie tried to work at home on Friday evening, but account sheets kept blurring before her eyes as her thoughts strayed. Several times she caught herself listening for the click of toenails on the kitchen linoleum. The apartment seemed too empty now without Callie.

She put a Streisand tape on the stereo and turned it low, but the mellow music failed to have its usual lulling effect, probably because the lyrics had to do with empty arms and midnight tears.

She tossed her pen aside and raked her fingers through her hair. Did it really matter if she waited until next week to make more collection calls? Was collecting for the savings and loan so darned urgent that she had to harass delinquent debtors on the weekend? No, she decided.

She stacked the account folders and left the desk. Going into the kitchen, she poured a glass of red wine and carried it back to the living room. She turned off the stereo in the middle of a throat-clutching tune about longing for yesterday's love. Then she kicked off her shoes and settled in a corner of the couch, her feet tucked beneath her.

Usually she enjoyed spending her Friday evenings alone, catching up on laundry and housework, curling up with a good book. But not tonight.

Yet it was a typical Friday evening, much like most of the previous ones over the past year. So why do I feel so lonely? she wondered.

Wired with nervous energy after arriving home from Sam's, she had thrown herself into a two-hour cleaning binge. Glancing around her now, she hardly recognized the apartment. Wood gleamed with lemon oil. The patch of linoleum she could see through the open kitchen doorway glowed with wax. All of her clothes hung on neatly aligned hangers in the bedroom closet. Her shoes, except for the loafers she'd just shed, were lined up on the closet floor. Her laundry had been washed, dried and put away. The problem with housework, she mused, was that you were always having to do it over.

At the moment, though, no household chores awaited her, and the office work could wait until Monday. She'd earned a relaxing evening at home.

"So relax," she murmured to herself.

The wine slid down her throat smoothly, creating a pleasant warmth in her body. It should have been the best hour of the week, but she found no enjoyment in it.

She missed Callie, of course, but mainly she missed Sam. After the past two days, spending a quiet evening at home alone had lost its appeal.

Odd that what one took pleasure in could change so abruptly. It suddenly occurred to Annie that she was in a melancholy mood because *she* had changed so abruptly. In the past two days she had let down the guards and become herself. She had, she realized, always been completely herself only with Sam.

She'd kept her innate sensuality hidden from everyone but Sam. After the breakup, she had even managed to hide the extent of her heartache. She hadn't been able to confide in friends—they all pointed out that, after all, ending the relationship had been *her* choice.

She hadn't confided in her parents, either. They loved her unconditionally, but she'd never wanted to disappoint them or see them hurt. So she'd always tried not to burden them with anything that would bring them disappointment or pain. Knowing that she was miserable made them miserable, so Annie had kept her desperate unhappiness over Sam to herself.

Nor did her parents suspect that her work had become her life since she'd left Sam. They had no idea how many invitations from friends she'd turned down in favor of staying late at the office, or that most of those friends had given up on her months ago.

Not that she had missed them all that much. The emptiness left in her life where Sam had been was all-encompassing, leaving no room for other losses. She had wanted only to crawl into a dark place, like a wounded animal, and be left alone to heal.

But the wounds still remained open and festering. If there had been any doubt about that, last night had certainly wiped it away. Nothing had changed, though, and she was back to square one. For her own protection, she had to keep some emotional distance between her and Sam.

Oh, perfect. Now if she could only figure out how to do that.

She swallowed the last of the wine and went to the kitchen for another glass. The kitchen wall clock ticked loudly in the quiet. 8:25. Much too early for bed.

Carrying her wineglass, Annie wandered back to the couch. Earlier today she had thought she needed time to think, but that didn't seem to be getting her anywhere except deeper into the doldrums. What good was thinking when she could be with Sam right now? Pride made a sorry companion.

Impulsively she reached for the phone. It rang beneath her hand.

"Annie?"

For that split second before lifting the receiver, she'd been sure it was Sam and her heart had leaped. Now she hoped her disappointment didn't come through in her voice. "Mom, hi."

"You okay, honey? You sound down." Her mother knew her too well.

"Just tired."

"I've tried to reach you a couple of times, but you weren't home. We've been expecting to hear from you. What did you find out in California?"

Heavens, she had forgotten to write. She'd known they would be curious, but seeing Sam again had knocked that and everything else out of her head. "I'm sorry, Mom. I've been so busy." She knew her mother would interpret Annie's busyness as an active social life; she'd been letting her do so for months.

"That's okay. I know how it is. So, tell me."

Perhaps it was hearing her mother's voice so unexpectedly. Perhaps it was the wine. Whatever it was, Annie forgot her resolve not to mention Sam and started talking. She told her mother about the inheritance and Sam's involvement in it. She told her about keeping Callie in the apartment and the landlord's ultimatum and leaving the dog at Sam's and the visit to the vet and Callie's surgery and how she wished she could keep Callie with her.

It all spilled out like a flood suddenly released by a collapsed levee. She held back nothing—except that she'd spent Thursday night in Sam's bed and that she still loved him, desperately.

When Annie ran down, her mother asked, "How do you feel about seeing Sam again?"

"I—I don't know."

"Oh, Annie. You still care for him." It wasn't a question. Indeed her mother knew her too well.

"Maybe," she admitted. "Don't worry, Mom. I'm a big girl. I can handle it."

"It might help to get out of town for a while. Why don't you schedule your vacation right away? We'll keep you so busy you won't have time to think about anything else."

"I can't come now, Mom. Somebody has to work with Callie, and Sam's out of town a lot. I guess I forgot to tell you that Callie's a TV star."

Annie's mother expressed her amazement, then called for Annie's father to pick up the other phone. They spent the next quarter of an hour in a three-way conversation, mostly about Callie's career. At least, Annie reflected, the news had taken her mother's mind off Sam.

By the time Annie hung up, she'd finished her second glass of wine. With her parents' voices still echoing in her mind, the apartment seemed less empty than before. She decided to take a long, hot bath and get to bed early. Sleep would be a welcome oblivion.

Saturday morning Annie called the clinic and was assured that Callie was recovering nicely from the surgery. When she didn't hear from Sam, she wondered what he was doing. Was he working on the house? Was he thinking of her? She wondered if his house felt as empty as hers.

Sunday was rainy and bleak, so Annie rented three scary movies at the video store. She immersed herself in Technicolor murder, mayhem and the tracking down of killers, but she couldn't lose herself enough to forget that Sam hadn't called all weekend.

Monday morning she arrived at work a half hour early, but not ahead of her boss. They were the only two people in the office who regularly arrived early. Annie made coffee and thrust her head into Layman's office to say, "'Morning, Harry. Coffee's made. Want a cup?''

Layman looked up from a pile of computer printouts. "Since when do you women libbers around here bring me coffee?" He was in an argumentative mood, Annie could tell. Probably still stewing over the run-in he'd had with one of the secretaries last week. When Layman had said he needed a refill on coffee, the secretary had responded sweetly, "No problem, Mr. Layman. There's still half a pot," and walked out, leaving Layman to get his own coffee.

Annie filled a Styrofoam cup and set it on Layman's desk. "Maybe we like to do the unexpected now and then. Keep you on your toes."

"You're trying to make up for leaving me in the lurch last week," Layman observed as he lifted the cup. He sipped and blanched. "Damn, that's hot." He set the cup down and glared at it as though burning his tongue was the coffee's fault.

Annie leaned one hip against the doorjamb. "You know, Harry, strange as it may seem to you, taking one day off from work for personal business isn't an act of disloyalty."

"You were late Wednesday morning, too, don't forget. I hope it isn't going to become a habit."

"God, Harry, you make Simon Legree look like a philanthropist. I explained about the dog...."

He waved her words aside. "I never heard of anybody else's dog taking up so much time."

Annie lifted her shoulders and sighed. Layman would argue with a post when he was in one of his moods. "I seem to remember your wife calling here about ten times the day her poodle had pups. You finally went home at noon, and you didn't come back until the next day."

"Mildred gets hysterical, but then she's not a career woman like you."

"This career is feeling more and more like just another dead-end job to me, Harry."

He stared at her, displeased because she had the
audacity to complain. "You have to position yourself
and be ready to grab the brass ring when it passes by,"
he snapped.

"I've had my hand up waiting for the brass ring so
long, my arm's paralyzed."

"I've told you you're in line for the next promotion—provided you don't start letting your work
slide."

Annie thought of the hours upon hours of overtime she'd put in lately, without any extra pay. Her job
description put her in the ranks of "management,"
and management employees worked for straight sal-
ary no matter how many hours of overtime the job
required. Annie had accepted that when she'd taken
the position. What galled her was Harry's disgrun-
tled attitude every time she wanted a few hours off.

"Promises, promises, Harry. You can only dangle
a carrot—or a brass ring—for so long before it loses
its appeal. By the way, you're welcome for the coffee." She left before he had time to frame a suitably
belligerent reply, but she heard him grumbling to
himself as she poured another cup of coffee and carried it to her office.

When Dana Fields, the receptionist, arrived at eight-
thirty, she stopped at Annie's open door to say good-
morning. "Missed you Friday," Dana said. "Are you
feeling better?"

Dana had worked at the savings and loan for about
a year. She was a pretty blonde in her early twenties
who acquired a new boyfriend about once a month.
Dana lived for evenings and weekends. Work was a
distasteful necessity. But, surprisingly, she managed to

give customers the impression that her goal in life was to make them happy, and she did it merely by smiling and chirping, "How may I help you?"

"I wasn't ill," Annie said.

Dana looked stumped for a moment. "But you never take off work unless you can't drag yourself out of bed. You have to be at death's door.... I thought—"

"I had to take my dog to the vet."

"I didn't know you even had a dog." She said it as though what she really meant was that she didn't know Annie had a *life* outside the office.

"It's a long, involved story, and not a particularly fascinating one."

Dana had a way of batting her false eyelashes that made her look like Little Miss Innocence fresh from convent school. She did it now, but Annie wasn't fooled. Dana had a sixth sense for uncovering any situation in which a man was even remotely involved.

"Sounds mysterious," Dana breathed. "You know what? You look different this morning."

"Different how?"

"Like, well, kind of unfocused. Like you've been shook up or something. You're usually so business-like, you know?"

Annie laughed. "Yes, I know."

"Dana!" Layman bellowed from his office. "It's too early for your coffee break—you just got here! Aren't you supposed to be at your desk?"

Dana raised her penciled brows. "Who rattled *his* cage?"

"Our fearless leader is in one of his surly moods this morning."

Dana groaned. "So what else is new? I guess I better go before he fires me." With obvious reluctance, she moved away from the door.

"Dana, what are you doing for lunch?" Annie called after her.

Dana popped back into the office, her green eyes wide and curious. "Say again?" Annie invariably sent out for a sandwich and ate it while she worked.

Her little altercation with Harry had made Annie feel rebellious. She hadn't really *liked* this job in months, she realized. Twice Harry had promised to get someone to assist her with collections, but as yet she saw no help on the horizon. Nor was she likely to. Besides being a perfect jerk, Harry lied.

"I have a craving for sweet-and-sour pork. Do you like Oriental food?"

"Love it."

"I've heard that Chinese restaurant in Penn Square is good. You game?"

"Well, sure." Dana was still staring at Annie as though she'd sprouted a second nose. The first few weeks Dana worked at the savings and loan, she'd asked Annie to go out for lunch with her almost every day. Once she'd even tried to fix Annie up with an ex-boyfriend. "He's really sweet," Dana had said. "There's just no chemistry there for me. He's real serious—kind of like you."

"At least you didn't say he has a great personality," Annie had said with a laugh. She'd turned down the date and the luncheon invitations. Obviously, Dana had finally decided Annie was hopeless, a boring nose-to-the-grindstone type.

"Good," Annie said now. "I'll tell you about my dog over lunch."

Maybe, Annie decided, she would even tell Dana about Sam. After all, whom did she know who had more experience with men than Dana?

But sharing confidences over lunch was not to be. When they arrived at the restaurant, Dana ran into an old boyfriend. Annie thought it possible that *most* men under thirty-five whom Dana ran into were ex-boyfriends. This one's name was Eddy, and Dana invited him to eat with them. She then proceeded to talk exclusively to Eddy as though Annie weren't there.

Watching her, Annie saw why Dana had so many boyfriends. She hung on every word that fell from Eddy's lips as though his conversation—about a sailboat he wanted to buy—was the most fascinating thing she'd ever heard. Whenever he paused, Dana smiled at him with her lashes lowered coquettishly. And she touched him almost constantly—his arms, his hand, his cheek. Lord knows what's going on under the table, Annie reflected.

Sighing inwardly, Annie quietly ate her sweet-and-sour pork and kept her confidences safely tucked away. You were crazy to cast Dana in a role of counselor in the first place, you dope, she told herself.

By eight o'clock Monday evening, Annie had decided to phone Sam. He obviously wasn't going to make contact with her, and she wanted to know how Callie was progressing. Also, she admitted to herself, she was starved for the sound of Sam's voice. Besides, she had to learn to talk to him without getting emotional. They were business partners now.

The phone rang five times before he answered.

"Hi, Sam. I hope I didn't take you away from something important."

"Hello, Annie. I was putting up wallboard. Didn't hear the phone." He sounded wonderful, not at all as though he'd been brooding and waiting for the phone to ring.

"Is Callie all right?"

"She was off her food for a couple of days, but her appetite's coming back now. That dog's got personality—no wonder the dog food company loves her. I'm actually starting to like having her around."

"I wish I could keep her here part of the time," Annie sighed. "I miss her."

"You know you can come out here whenever you want." His voice had become a bit tense.

Beneath his determinedly casual manner, Sam was still off balance about her abrupt departure Friday. They needed time to think, she'd said. Hell, what Sam *didn't* need was any more time to think about Annie. He'd spent too many hours so occupied already. Nothing ever came of it but a feeling of frustration.

After a strained silence Annie said, "Thank you, Sam. I'll keep that in mind."

Clearly, Annie didn't want to talk about Thursday night. "Doc Moses said not to let Callie do anything too strenuous for a few days," Sam said.

"I guess we should put off the training sessions until next week, then. I could come out Sunday afternoon and get started."

"Sunday would be good," Sam agreed. "I'll be away, and Callie will be glad for the company. I'll leave the house key in the cedar planter on the porch. Stay as long as you like.''

He sounded quite cheerful, as though he preferred her coming when he was gone. Where was he going? Annie wondered. It was just like Sam not to tell her anything more than the bare bones, but she wasn't about to ask him to elaborate. "Okay." She wasn't ready to hang up, but she couldn't think of anything else to say. Surely a first, Annie told herself. Usually her problem was that she said too much.

"Well . . . talk to you later. . . ."

"Wait," Sam said quickly, and Annie's heart lifted. Maybe Sam *had* missed her.

Sam *wanted* to say, "What's the all-fired hurry, Annie? Talk to me, dammit!" Instead he said, "I called L.A. this morning, talked to Smallwood about getting Barnes to turn over Callie's financial records. He'd already requested them."

Why had she imagined he was about to say something personal—like he wanted her, needed her? Get real, Annie.

"And?"

"Barnes sent copies of ledger sheets with handwritten entries. That in itself is suspicious. Almost everyone has their bookkeeping records on computer these days."

"You mean you think Barnes manufactured the records he sent Smallwood?"

"I think it's possible. At any rate, the auditor Smallwood turned the records over to is less than satisfied. They show that Callie earned about twenty thousand last year, but according to the contract with the dog food company, she gets about that for the tapings alone, and there should be residuals every time a commercial is aired. I left the television on while I was working on the house last weekend, and I heard Callie's commercial three times."

"Barnes must have been stealing Freddy blind. You know how Freddy was. He trusted everyone."

"Yeah."

"It makes me furious, thinking of Barnes taking advantage of poor, trusting Freddy. I'd like to sue his pants off."

"Smallwood has requested that Barnes allow an auditor in his office to go through the financial records. But if Barnes wants to fight us in court, which it seems likely he'll do, it could take years to get a look at all the records. And legal fees would kill us. Barnes probably keeps two sets of books, and he's too smart to leave incriminating records where they might be seen by the wrong eyes."

"Terrific," Annie muttered.

"There is a silver lining," Sam said. "The agency contract with Barnes is up for renewal in May, two weeks before the next taping session. We have to give him thirty days' notice of intention not to renew."

"I think we should do it."

"I agree. I'll send a certified letter. Do you want to read it before I mail it?"

"That's not necessary, Sam. But how do we find another agent?"

"I'll check around. Maybe Smallwood will have a suggestion."

Unfortunately the empty ache in the region of Annie's heart hadn't been eased by hearing Sam's voice on the telephone. Maybe if she could see him . . . But

Sam wasn't likely to suggest that. He'd issued an invitation for Friday night, and she'd turned him down. Now it was her move.

Impulsively she said in a rush, "I want to repay you for dinner Thursday. Would you like to have dinner here tomorrow night?"

For a long moment no sound came from the other end of the line, not even the sound of Sam's breathing. Finally he said, "I'm sorry, Annie. I'm not free tomorrow."

Not free. What did that mean? Did he have another date? If he really wanted to see her, he could easily have suggested another night. But he waited, saying nothing more. She'd been a fool to ask.

"No problem," Annie managed. "I'm not a very good cook, anyway, as you know." She took a deep breath before adding, "Gotta go. I'll see you ... when I see you. Bye, Sam."

Sam heard a click and then the dial tone. He stared at nothing for an instant before replacing the receiver. He should have explained that he had a business meeting tomorrow night, but Annie's invitation had surprised him. Was she having second thoughts about keeping the distance between them that she'd said she wanted? With Annie, you never knew. Sometimes she went from one end of the pole to the other, without warning.

More likely, it was exactly as she'd said. She felt she owed him dinner because of the meal he'd fixed on Thursday night. He hated game playing, and he wanted nothing from Annie if it came from a sense of obligation.

Slowly he left the kitchen and, with Callie at his heels, went out to the deck. He didn't feel like working anymore tonight, so he stretched out on a chaise. Callie rested her head on his thigh and looked up at him with her sad basset hound eyes. He caressed a floppy ear absently.

He wanted to shake Annie. No—he wanted her, period. Why did she have to make things so complicated? Hell, he might as well ask why he couldn't have fallen for a less-complicated woman.

He closed his eyes and saw Annie as she looked when they made love, skin flushed, eyes a bit dazed and as dark as midnight.

Take me to your bed. I want you, Sam.

His fingers tightened on Callie's ear; Sam was unaware of it until the dog whined mournfully. Then he forced himself to relax. "Sorry, old girl," he muttered.

I need you so much.

Had those been mere words? Had she even known what she was saying?

Oh, Sam...

Everything had seemed fine until he suggested she spend the night again. Then, wham, just like that, she withdrew from him. Had he asked in the wrong way? God knew he wasn't great with words. If he had been, he might have gone into criminal law instead of corporate. Maybe it was the tone of voice he'd used. Had he given Annie the impression he was taking it for granted that she would stay? Annie didn't like being taken for granted, that he knew.

Feeling his frustration building, Sam rose and, dragging a hand through his hair, went back inside.

Wearing himself out with physical labor was the only way he was going to get to sleep tonight. He went back to the unfinished part of the house, picked up his hammer and started pounding.

Seven

On Sunday, Annie found Callie fully recovered and ecstatic about seeing her again. When Callie finally stopped squirming with delight and barking in reply to everything Annie said, Annie walked through Sam's spotless house, noting that two of the unfinished rooms now had wallboard installed, and that the walls and ceilings were ready for paper or paint.

She continued back through the house to Sam's bedroom where the faint scent of Sam's after-shave set off a flurry of vivid memories of the last time she'd been there. She ran her hand over the smooth quilted bedspread as though to absorb the warmth left by Sam's body.

In the adjoining bathroom, tile, tub and basins sparkled, faucets gleamed. Thirsty, chocolate-colored towels hung in perfect alignment on their racks. Toiletries were placed in orderly arrangement on the glass shelves of the mirror-doored medicine cabinet. The soft click as Annie closed the medicine cabinet door was loud in the silent room.

Callie watched Annie curiously, her head cocked to one side as though trying to figure out what Annie was doing. What *am* I doing? Annie wondered.

At that point, Annie realized she was looking for some evidence that a woman had been there since her last visit. *Annie Malloy, you are pathetic.* Turning away in self-disgust, she walked purposefully back to the living room.

Callie, following at Annie's heels, looked up at her and barked, as if to say, "Enough of this pointless meandering." Annie laughed and hugged the dog. "I didn't mean to ignore you, girl. Come on, let's go out to the yard. Your vacation is over. We're getting down to business."

Annie worked with the dog for more than an hour, going through Callie's repertoire of tricks again and again. The dog seemed a bit rusty at first, but she soon was preforming on command. Annie then taught her to fetch an old tennis ball she'd found in the garage. The command was obviously new to Callie, but she learned it quickly.

"You've earned a treat," Annie said at last. They went back inside, and Annie rummaged through Sam's refrigerator. She found some American cheese slices, which Callie loved, and gave her two. She knew that what Callie would like more than anything, though, was a good, long run. So she snapped on Callie's leash and they trotted along the country road for about a mile before turning back.

Sam didn't return before Annie left. As she drove back to town, Annie couldn't help wondering if Sam had made it a point to stay away until he was sure she would be gone.

Monday morning, Annie phoned L.A. to see if Freddy's attorney, Smallwood, had been able to get any more records from Barnes. "Barnes says he's already sent all he has," Smallwood said. "He was furious about a letter he received from Mr. Bennington."

"Sam terminated Barnes's contract," Annie said. "We're looking for another agent. I thought Sam might have contacted you about it."

"I haven't heard from him."

"I guess he's been too busy with other things. Anyway, it doesn't look as if we're going to get any more information from Barnes without a court order."

"That's my reading of the situation," Smallwood said.

"I'd like to talk to somebody at the dog food company then. Could you write and inform them that Callie has new owners and will be getting a new agent? And let them know that I'll be contacting them soon?"

"I'll get a letter off today, Miss Malloy."

Annie hung up, feeling that Sam would probably be better able to handle the business with the dog food company. But she was reluctant to dump everything in his lap. Besides, Sam didn't seem to feel they had anything to talk about. She hadn't heard from him in a week.

Annie went to Sam's place again late Tuesday afternoon to work with Callie and ran into Jude Preston, who was returning Callie to Sam's yard after taking her for a walk. Bud was with him, of course.

For once Preston didn't seem to have been drinking. Bud greeted Annie like a long-lost friend, oblivious to the worry he'd put her through over Callie.

"Sam told me you might come out," Jude said to Annie. "I've been feeding and walking Callie while he's out of town."

Sam might, at least, have informed her that he was leaving town, Annie thought. "When's he coming back?"

"Next week sometime. I'll take good care of Callie, though. You don't need to worry about her."

Annie agreed not to worry, but the next two evenings she went out to work with Callie, putting her through a quick training session and then staying a couple more hours to keep her company. She liked the feeling of being in Sam's house, or sitting on his deck with Callie as evening dusk darkened into night, locusts droned and an owl hooted from a nearby tree. She felt serene and, in a strange way, protected.

Upon leaving Sam's house Thursday night, Annie warned herself not to like it *too* much.

Sam had been obliged to fly to Denver unexpectedly. He'd had no opportunity to let Annie know of his departure before he left. After checking in at the Denver hotel, he'd reached for the phone several times to call her. But each time he'd had second thoughts. What was the point? What could he say to her that would make any difference?

* * *

Friday morning, a few minutes after the savings and loan opened for business, Harry Layman stomped into Annie's office with an agitated customer.

"Annie, this is Mr. Dunwiller—Abbott Dunwiller. Do you have his file?"

"Yes, er, good morning, Mr. Dunwiller."

She knew the name well. Dunwiller's mortgage payments were four months in arrears. She had failed repeatedly to reach him by phone, both at work and at home. Several times she'd had the strong feeling that his secretary and his wife were lying when they said he was out. Finally, on Tuesday, she'd mailed a certified letter, reminding him that a bad report to the credit bureau could damage his credit rating for years, asking him to make up the back payments at once and warning that "more drastic measures" to collect the money owed to the savings and loan would be instituted should he fail to comply.

Dunwiller did not respond to Annie's greeting. He stood there rigidly, arms folded across his chest, while she shuffled through the folders on her desk and came up with the right file. She handed it to Harry, who scanned it impatiently.

"No payments have been posted to this account since December 30," Layman said, frowning at Annie.

Annie didn't like his accusatory manner. "That's because no payments have been made since that date," she said.

"That's a lie!" Dunwiller thundered.

The man's loud voice in the small office made Annie jump. Dunwiller was lying through his teeth. She tried to keep a rein on her temper. "Let me rephrase that. No payments have been received in this office since that date."

"Then they were lost in the mail!" Dunwiller snapped.

Annie glanced at Layman, her dark brows lifted in disbelief. Layman said nothing. "Mr. Dunwiller," Annie said, "the post office might conceivably misplace one payment, even two. But four?"

"She's calling me a liar," Dunwiller said to Layman. "Did you hear her?"

"Now, I don't think that's what Miss Malloy meant. Annie, Mr. Dunwiller is a valued customer."

Annie stared at her boss. How could he take the side of this deadbeat? Layman was a petty tyrant around the office, but when it came to someone over whom he had no authority, his backbone turned to spaghetti. The weasel!

Dunwiller planted his big hands on Annie's desk and leaned toward her. His face was red and he was wheezing. His blood pressure must be sky-high, Annie reflected. "On second thought," Dunwiller said, "maybe the post office isn't to blame. Maybe my checks were diverted after they reached the savings and loan."

Annie darted a glance at Layman. The dolt just stood there. She glimpsed Dana Fields and one of the secretaries hovering in the reception area, taking in every word. In fact, everyone in the building must be listening; Layman hadn't bothered to close the office door. The employees would have a bit of juicy gossip to occupy them during the morning coffee break.

Feeling at a disadvantage with Dunwiller looming over her, Annie rose to her feet. "I resent your implication, Mr. Dunwiller."

"Now, Annie..."

Dunwiller ignored Layman. "Not half as much as I resent getting that threatening letter out of the blue!"

"It was hardly out of the blue," Annie responded. "I've been leaving messages at your office and home for weeks. You haven't seen fit to get back to me."

"I'm getting the hell back to you right now!" Dunwiller shouted. "What kind of bookkeeping procedures do you have around here, Layman? I demand an apology!"

"We'll get this straightened out, I'm sure," Layman said soothingly.

Annie's telephone rang. "Mr. Dunwiller, if you'll just send us copies of the canceled checks, showing that you've made the payments—" she reached for the phone "—I'll be more than happy to apologize." She brought the receiver to her ear. "Miss Malloy speaking."

"Annie?"

"Sam!"

"I wouldn't put up with such insubordination from an employee of mine," Dunwiller was saying. "You give some people a little authority and it goes to their head. I'm being harassed by this woman!"

Annie sent Layman a glance, pleading with him to get Dunwiller out of her office. "Where are you calling from, Sam?"

"Denver." The pull of the telephone in Sam's hotel room had finally overcome his misgivings. "I didn't have a chance to let you know before I left town. Too many things piling up on me at once.''

"I understand. I ran into Jude out at your place. He told me you were out of town."

"You've been training Callie?"

"Yes. She's a snap to work with."

Dunwiller was still complaining in the background, and Layman was trying to defuse his anger by groveling. "What's all that racket?" Sam asked.

"I have somebody in my office—"

Dunwiller drowned her out. "I won't stand here and be insulted!"

"Miss Malloy," Layman said, *"will you please get off that phone!"*

"Sam, I can't talk now. I'm really sorry." Annie murmured a hasty goodbye and hung up.

"You'll be hearing from my lawyer!" Having delivered his parting shot, Dunwiller stomped out of the office, storming through the reception area and flinging open the two glass entry doors as he swept through.

Annie sighed and sank back into her chair. "Do you know who he is?" Layman asked, agitated.

"Abbott Dunwiller."

"Of *the* Dunwillers," Layman said. "Dunwiller Drilling Company. He plays golf with the chairman of our board."

"He's still four months behind on his mortgage payments," Annie said. "Harry, he's into the savings and loan for more than half a million. Maybe you should check on the status of Dunwiller Drilling. It could well be another petroleum-related company on the verge of bankruptcy."

Layman stared hard at her for an instant. "Are you sure there's no mistake in the records?"

"Absolutely."

"You'd better be right," Layman said, "because if you're not..." He left the threat hanging.

"Thanks for the vote of confidence, Harry."

Layman grumbled an oath and left the office. Annie closed her door. She sat back down at the desk and held her head in her hands. Did Harry really think she was so incompetent as to have misplaced four mortgage payments? Of course he didn't, damn him. Dunwiller had influence in high places, and Harry wanted to make certain Annie took whatever heat might come down.

Oh, God, of all times for Sam to call—when she hadn't heard from him in two weeks, and she'd been longing to hear his voice. But she'd been so distracted by Dunwiller that she'd cut Sam off rudely. She had to phone him back and apologize.

Annie lifted her head and stared at the telephone. She couldn't phone Sam. She hadn't even asked where he was staying.

During the next few days Annie tried to drive thoughts of Sam out of her head with work. Dunwiller had not sent copies of canceled checks, for as Annie pointed out to Layman, it was difficult to get copies of checks that didn't exist. Nor did they hear from Dunwiller's lawyer.

"We won't do anything about it yet," Layman told Annie. "Let it ride for now."

"Fine," Annie said, and handed him Dunwiller's file. "You decide how much slack he's going to get, and then you handle it."

She worked with Callie both Saturday and Sunday afternoons. At home, she waited to hear from Sam again. He didn't call.

On Monday, Annie phoned the dog food company and was put through to Suzanne Corbet in marketing. Smallwood had paved the way for her call, and Suzanne was warm and informative. As Annie and Sam had suspected, Callie's earnings for the past year, according to the dog food company's accounts, were considerably more than Barnes's records showed.

Annie asked that all future correspondence be mailed to her and Sam until they had decided on a new agent for Callie. She had just hung up when she received a phone call from Smallwood. Barnes had miraculously discovered the "misplaced" records. The new figures more or less jibed with those given to Annie by Suzanne Corbet.

"Unfortunately," Smallwood said, "Barnes says he paid it all out to Freddy."

"Which we can't disprove," Annie said.

"I found no receipt records when I went through Mr. Malloy's things," Smallwood agreed.

"We can't even sue Barnes for fraud," Annie said. "His figures agree with the dog food company's. Why do you think he lied before?"

Smallwood hesitated for a long moment. "This is off the record, Miss Malloy, but it occurred to me that as long as Barnes thought he would continue as Callie's agent, he didn't want you and Mr. Bennington to know how much the dog would be earning in the future. Then, of course, he received Mr. Bennington's letter terminating the contract.''

''You mean he planned to go on stealing from us, the way he stole from Freddy, if we were stupid enough to take his word,'' Annie muttered.

''You said that, not I, Miss Malloy. We have no proof.''

''Yes, I know,'' Annie sighed. ''Thank you for calling, Mr. Smallwood.''

When Annie drove out to work with Callie late Tuesday afternoon, the sight of Sam's car in the driveway sent a stab of uncertainty through her. She got out of her car slowly, wishing she'd known he was home so she could have prepared herself. As it was, she felt stupidly flustered.

Sam watched her approach the house. He'd arrived home two hours ago and after feeding Callie and putting her in the yard, he'd eaten a sandwich. Now, seated in the big armchair in his bedroom with his legs stretched out, he studied her from behind partially opened miniblinds.

She's beautiful, he mused, watching the way the red fabric of her slacks molded to her thighs as she came slowly up the front walk. Two years ago he'd thought she was cute, vibrant, sexy. For perhaps the first time he realized that all of those things and more had combined into true beauty.

She was older now, for one thing—she'd be twenty-nine in a couple of months. And perhaps in some way, the months of their separation had given her a new maturity. If emotional pain had contributed to its development, then he was more mature, as well. Certainly, he was more cautious.

His face clouded a moment. With an effort, he forced the frown from his expression. This wasn't the time to think about those miserable months or to dwell on why she'd recently come to his bed so eagerly only to pull away from him again the next day. Or to imagine that she'd had more reason than a customer in her office to cut him off so abruptly when he'd finally stopped vacillating and called her from Denver.

How did she really feel about him? If some love remained to build on, could he give her what she needed this time, something he hadn't been able to give her before? And did he dare risk being vulnerable again? So many questions crowded his mind.

Yet he recognized that she'd learned to be cautious, too, in a way that she had never been before. He would respect that. He would take his cues from her and wait for what would be. He no longer kidded himself that he would be the one to walk out this time. But before he let her leave him again, he'd know if, in some remote corner of her heart, she loved him still.

In stepping up to the porch, she passed out of his line of vision. He quickly levered himself to his feet by gripping the arms of his chair and went to answer the doorbell.

He swung the door open. "Greetings, Miss Malloy."

She caught her tongue between her teeth and studied him. In jeans and a brown T-shirt, he looked relaxed, but there were tired lines at the corners of his eyes. "The wanderer has returned."

"Did I ever mention how much I hate hotel rooms?" He held the glass storm door open for her. The scent of her perfume floated to him as she entered the house.

"I don't believe so."

He followed her into the living room. She stood near the French doors and watched Callie chasing a ball around the yard. She seemed tense. "They either smell like stale tobacco or reek of pine deodorizer. And the pillows are flat."

She turned around and thrust her hands into the pockets of her slacks. Her white shirt opened in a V in front, exposing the smooth, ivory skin of her throat and a shadow hinting at the beginning of cleavage. "I'm sorry for hanging up on you when you called the office. I wanted to call you back, but I didn't know where you were staying."

She could have gotten that information from his office, Sam reflected, but he didn't ask why she hadn't. Maybe he preferred to believe she hadn't thought of it. "It sounded as though you were trying to deal with a customer problem."

"A problem customer." She shook her hair back and wandered restlessly to the bookcase to finger the spine of an atlas.

His eyes followed the line of her back, down past the slender waist to the curve of her derriere. His hands itched to go where his gaze rested. He wrenched his eyes upward and sank into a chair, stretching his legs out in front of him. "Sit down, Annie."

She turned her head and caught the look in Sam's eyes as they settled on her mouth. She moistened her lips with the tip of her tongue. "I'm too itchy to sit."

"I noticed," he said softly, dragging his eyes away from her mouth. When his gaze met hers, he read confusion there. A faint flush colored her pale cheeks. At least the sexual attraction is still strong, he mused with a grim sort of satisfaction. But the satisfaction was fleeting. The physical attraction had always been there, right up until the day she'd left him.

Seized with a jittery need to move, Annie walked to the fireplace and propped one foot on the low hearth. "I came to work with Callie, but we need to talk first."

That part of her hadn't changed, Sam thought. Annie had always had an insatiable need to talk. He, on the other hand, would have much preferred to pull her down on his lap and kiss her until she was breathless with wanting him.

"What about?"

"First, Barnes came through with the financial records—after he received your certified letter. They seem to jibe with what I learned from the dog food company—I had a long conversation with someone there, by the way. Barnes says he paid out every cent owed to Freddy. Since Freddy evidently kept no records, we're stuck with his word."

"I really didn't expect there'd be any money coming to us, did you?"

"No, I just feel Barnes is lying. The first records he sent Smallwood—when he still thought he would be representing Callie for us—showed less income than the later records do. He wanted our future expectations to be based on the lower figure. Evidently he thought we were a couple of yokels who wouldn't question him."

"We fired him, Annie. It doesn't matter what he thinks."

She left the fireplace and went to stand in front of the French doors. "I told Suzanne Corbet, the woman I talked to at the dog food company, that we'd notify her when we found a new agent for Callie. I told her to send all correspondence to us in the meantime." She flexed her shoulders as though in an effort to relax tight muscles, then dropped them again. She lifted her hair off the back of her neck with both hands, then walked over and straightened a picture on the wall.

Sam watched this display of nerves, only half hearing what she was saying because all he wanted to do was touch her. What made him hesitate was a nagging fear that she'd come to regret the night of intimacy they'd shared two weeks ago. She seemed determined to keep the conversation on business. He closed his eyes for a moment, but her image was imprinted on the backs of his eyelids. Was he a fool to have let himself get involved with her again?

"Sam!" She stood in the center of the room, staring at him. "Have you heard anything I've said?"

He looked up at her thoughtfully. "Sort of."

"You're tired. I should have checked to see if you were home before I came. You aren't expecting someone, are you? If you are, I'll get out of your way."

"I'm not expecting anyone."

She gazed at him uncertainly. "I suppose I should have consulted you before contacting the dog food company. You think it was presumptuous of me, don't you?"

Sam came to his feet slowly. "I don't give a damn about that, Annie."

She caught her lip between her teeth and smiled faintly. "We need to talk about getting an agent, Sam."

"I'm still working on it, but let's not talk about that now," he murmured as he crossed the room.

Annie's look was confused. "But—" The word was hardly out of her mouth when he pulled her against him, his mouth claiming hers. Bewilderment and desire rose in her as, hardly aware of what she was doing, she clung to him.

"I want you, Annie," he mumbled against her mouth. "I missed you like hell."

Annie's head swam and her heart was beating too rapidly. She drew back a little to try to steady herself. What was he saying? He couldn't possibly know what it was to really miss someone, to be literally sick with longing. She should have turned around and gone back to town as soon as she'd seen he was home. She couldn't handle this.

"Missed me?" she whispered unsteadily. "Oh, Sam, you don't have to lie to me to get me into bed." She swallowed hard to force back a sob. "I—I resent it—it's demeaning."

Sam stiffened, his fingers gripping her shoulders painfully. The admission had been wrenched from him against his will, and she didn't believe him! Could she really not know how desperately he needed her? God, could he do nothing right with Annie?

He was unable to check the impulse to hurt her in return. "Don't talk to me about lies, Annie," he said, holding himself with rigid control. "You can lie with your body as well as with words."

Annie stared at him, wounded. Why *did* he think she'd made love with him? Did he really believe she'd had any control at that moment, that she'd had some devious plan in mind? "I haven't heard from you in two weeks! If you missed me so much, why didn't you call me from Denver?"

"I did. You hung up on me."

"I explained that! Oh, Sam . . . I waited and waited for you to call back."

"How was I supposed to know that? I'm not a mind reader, dammit."

Annie wanted to say that *he* was the one who had always expected her to read his mind. *He* was the one who kept things inside. But what was the use? She'd tried to tell him that fifteen months ago.

His convulsive grip on her shoulders eased. "God, Annie, I've waited for days to be alone with you. Now that I am, we can't do anything but hurt each other."

"Like old times, right?" Annie said, and her eyes misted. Her fingers, as if with a will of their own, traced the stubborn line of his jaw. She would *not* drag up all that pain tonight. "Let's stop hurting each other for one night, Sam." Her voice was husky, and with sudden urgency she tugged at his shirt. "Just kiss me. Please."

Passion engulfed them with staggering swiftness. Sam's hunger grew as hers matched it and kept pace. No matter how much they hurt each other, she had always been soft and eager for his lovemaking. Had he been an eloquent man, he might have told her how much that thrilled him, how easily she could bring him to his knees, how at moments such as this he was in awe of her and frightened by the depth of the feeling.

But he was not eloquent. Even if he had been, the driving power of their passion would have made expressing such grand thoughts impossible.

With clumsy haste, their clothing was disposed of. Slacks, shirts, shoes were flung aside to lie wherever they chanced to fall. The gray velvet hush of evening deepened beyond the glass wall of the room as they savored each other. The wild glory of pure, primitive desire surrounded and filled them. He smelled of soap and shampoo from his recent shower. The scent of her perfume made him dizzy, and the warm, sweet taste of her mouth inflamed him.

When no remaining barrier of clothing separated them, they lay together on the carpet in front of the massive stone fireplace, their bodies hot and moist and pulsing with need. Hands wandered restlessly in their eagerness to reclaim each familiar curve and line and angle. Their breath came quick and fast. The sounds they made were soft, guttural murmurings of pleasure.

The caress of his hands on her flesh made Annie tremble. Her open mouth pressed against his neck, the hard curve of his shoulder, the base of his throat. Her mouth was wet, her breath warm on his skin, and Sam's senses reeled.

He rolled her over and beneath him so that he could find the rich, heady taste of the damp skin beneath her breasts. He trailed kisses down over her flat stomach, and she shuddered convulsively beneath him.

She groaned and arched into him, wanting, seeking, and the strength of Sam's passion was so great that it frightened him. He tried to hold back, fearing hazily that he might crush her with his hardness and need, fearing that he might bruise her without even knowing.

But she had no patience with his restraint. She uttered little gasps of pleading and her hands were hot as they drew him to her.

Sam forgot control. Desperation took over. Reason fled, overwhelmed by need so strong it verged on insanity. He felt as though he'd plunged into the eye of a hurricane. The savage winds howled all around him. He thrust into her and rode with the storm as it buffeted him mercilessly, pounding in him with a wild, frenzied rhythm.

Then, in the instant when he thought his laboring heart would burst from his chest, he was flung ashore in an explosion of shattering release and swift, indescribable pleasure.

Eight

They were spent. Annie lay on her back on the carpet, her arms cradling Sam's head, which nestled between her breasts. It was completely dark now beyond the big panes of glass, and a full moon bathed the room and their bodies in silver. Annie felt swaddled in lazy contentment. She closed her eyes and hugged the feeling to her.

Why did it always seem at moments such as this that nothing else mattered, that there was no problem too hard for them to overcome together? Yet, when there was time for reflection, the obstacles seemed insurmountable. But Annie didn't want to think about the obstacles quite yet. Not while her flesh still glowed and her muscles still trembled with the weakness left by sated passion.

No matter how often they made love, it was always new; the emotions and sensations now were as shattering in their strength as they had been the first time. Annie didn't think it could ever be that way with anyone else. Was it really true that for every woman there was only one absolutely right man in all the world? The thought was almost frightening.

"I feel like I weigh a ton," Sam said. "Am I squashing you?"

Annie toyed with the hair at the nape of his neck. "The carpet's scratching my bottom."

He chuckled, kissing the damp spot between her breasts before rolling off her. Rising, he lifted her and carried her to the couch. "Don't move. I'll be right back."

Annie curled contentedly into the soft cushions. "I couldn't move if I wanted to," she murmured.

Sam was back in a moment with a sheet, which he spread over them as he joined her on the couch. He drew her close and cradled her head on the curve of his shoulder. "Asleep?"

"No," Annie sighed and cuddled against him. "I was thinking about how wonderful I feel when we make love. Sex is amazing, isn't it?" She knew it was more than sex, so much more. She snuggled closer. "Mmm, I like this part, too. It's so warm and cozy with the sheet."

He stroked her thigh and drew her leg over him. "You always wanted a cover after we made love."

"It makes me feel secure."

He laughed and kicked the sheet off his feet. "I remember times when my blood was still so hot I thought I'd catch fire if the covers touched me."

"What else do you remember?"

He wrapped one of Annie's curls around his finger. "That you always wanted to talk afterward—you wanted to talk half the night."

"And you usually fell asleep in the middle of a sentence," she said defensively, causing him to plant a tender kiss on the top of her head.

They fell silent then, both knowing they had approached the crux of the dilemma that had eventually driven Annie away. Saying that Annie needed to talk about her feelings while Sam would sooner stand on a street corner naked than bare the depths of his soul was too simple. It was the reasons behind those tendencies and the way they—especially Annie—felt about this difference between them that had destroyed their relationship.

Communication on every level was so important to Annie that when Sam held things back, it meant that he didn't *trust* her fully. She *needed* to talk to him about everything and anything. The notion that he evidently didn't feel the same need translated in Annie's mind to Sam's not needing *her*.

What Annie never understood, and what Sam had not known how to reveal to her, was that he'd been more open with her than with anybody else ever before. He'd let himself love her, and that had made him vulnerable. Then she'd left him, and it had seemed like the worst kind of betrayal. It had nearly destroyed him, and he'd told himself that he would never run the risk of opening up to anyone again.

But what if keeping that promise made to himself in the blackness of despair meant the difference between having Annie in his life and losing her again?

She sighed and moved softly against him. "You asleep, Sam?"

"Uh-uh."

She planted a soft kiss on his chest where dark, springy hairs grew in the rough shape of a triangle and tapered to a thin line above his navel. "I think I'll skip Callie's session tonight. I should be getting home."

His hand tightened on her thigh, keeping her there. "You have a hot date or something?"

She raised up on one elbow to look at him. In the moonlight his face was all angles and shadows, the face of a god cast in silver. A faint smile touched his lips.

She tossed her head to fling tangled curls from her eyes. "I wouldn't say hot," she teased.

His brows lowered. "What would you say?"

"Faintly warm?"

"I'll kill him," he said matter-of-factly.

Annie smiled and moved so that she lay partially on top of him. She dropped her head to his shoulder and sighed. After a moment Sam said, "You were kidding about having a date, weren't you?"

She wrapped an arm around his waist. "Yes."

He slid his hand up to cup her hip. They lay like that for several moments. Finally, Sam asked, "Aren't you going to ask me what I'm thinking?"

"No."

"But you always ask me what I'm thinking."

"I promised myself I wouldn't start up with you tonight."

His fingers floated across her hip and up the smooth line of her back to nestle among the curls at the nape of her neck. "Maybe I could change, Annie."

She lay very still against him, hardly breathing. "Do you honestly think so?"

"I could try."

She tilted her head back and kissed his chin. "That's sweet of you, Sam. When do you plan to start?"

He took a deep breath. "No time like the present. Go ahead," he said. "Which of my dark secrets do you want to know? Ask me anything."

"Tell me about your childhood. How old were you when your parents separated?"

Well, he had said anything. He couldn't change his mind now. He took a deep breath. "Eight. I came home from school one day and my mother was gone. She cleared out her closet, took everything. Didn't even leave a note."

"Eight? Oh, Sam, you were hardly more than a baby."

"It scared the living daylights out of me." He had, in fact, been sure that his mother had died while he was at school and that someone had taken her away before he could see her. "I went to a neighbor's house, and she called my father at work. We were living in Wichita Falls at the time. We moved a lot when I was a kid. A couple of months after that, my father took a job in Oklahoma City and we moved again."

He had needed his father to talk to him about what had happened, to reassure him that, at least, his father would never leave him. Instead his father had retreated into black silence.

"Didn't your mother write you or call you, after she left?"

"We never heard from her again."

The words were stark and cold in the darkness. Annie had an urge to cradle him in her arms like a hurting child.

"And your father never remarried?"

"No. He—he got in with a hard-drinking bunch at the factory where he worked. They stopped at a bar every day after work. Stayed there for hours sometimes, drinking."

"What were you doing while he was at the bar?"

"I learned to entertain myself," Sam said simply. "I read and I learned to use my father's old carpentry tools. There was a dump not far from where we lived. I went there once or twice a week and picked up any pieces of lumber I could carry home."

Annie could see him, a sad, lonely little boy, scavenging for scraps of wood, lugging them home to build things while he wondered what he had done to make his parents abandon him. She couldn't speak. She wanted to cry.

"As soon as I was old enough, I worked as a carpenter's helper on weekends and school vacations. That's how I paid for college and law school."

Sam had stated the facts succinctly, but they didn't begin to cover the terror and guilt and impotent anger he'd felt. After a lengthy silence, he added softly, "My father died of cirrhosis of the liver when I was fourteen, and I went to a foster home. To ten, in fact, in the next four years. I wasn't an easy kid to live with. I was mad at the world."

And determined not to need anybody, Annie thought, determined not to let anybody get close enough to hurt him ever again. In some corner of his heart, that little boy was still there. "Sam—" Annie's voice broke. "I'm so very sorry."

"I don't want you to cry," he said. "You asked and I told you. It was a long time ago."

But it still hurt, Annie sensed. It hurt him to recall it, to talk about it. And that's what she had asked of him. Reaching up, she drew his head down to her. She kissed him softly, lingeringly.

"Is that for being a nice boy and spilling my guts?" he asked a bit self-deprecatingly.

"That," she whispered huskily, "is for being handsome and sexy and wonderful."

Shaking off bleak memories, he shifted and pulled her full on top of him. He nuzzled his lips against her throat. "I think you're kinda special, too."

"Truly?" She moved sinuously against him, rubbing her breasts against his soft mat of chest hair. "Tell me more." She moved her thigh against his.

He chuckled and molded his hand to the side of her breast. "Your desire for words is insatiable, woman. Okay, you asked for it. Hmm...your eyes are like pools—dark, muddy pools. Your skin is the color of buttermilk."

"Wow, what a way with the language."

Laughing, he rolled over and tumbled them both to the floor. Then he sat up, fearing that he'd hurt her. But she lay naked in the moonlight, her body touched magically with silver and surrounded by the pale carpet. Her hair was a dark halo around her face. Her eyes were black and half-closed. She smiled at him invitingly.

"Enough of this poetic stuff, Bennington. Let's see some action."

Desire, sudden and sharp, hit him like a fist and drove the breath from his lungs. He reached for her as she extended her arms to him.

Together, they found paradise.

Some time later Annie sat up beside him. "I'm going to have friction burns all over my body from this darned carpet."

He lay sprawled on his back, looking up at her with drowsy eyes. He didn't want to move. "We should have gone to bed."

"We didn't have time."

He grinned. "That's true."

She rose to her feet in a single, graceful movement. She stood, hands on hips, looking down at him. "Do you have anything to eat around here? I'm starved."

He groaned. "What would you like?"

She considered it. "An omelet would be nice. Make mine with cheese and onions. I'm going to take a quick shower."

He watched her shadowy form disappear completely into the dark hall. "You bet," he said, yawning hugely. He dragged himself to his feet and pulled on his discarded jeans. Automatically he began picking up the scattered pieces of clothing, then decided to hell with it, and dropped them again.

He walked barefoot to the kitchen and flipped the light switch, wincing as brightness flooded the room. "Dear God, I'm blinded."

He trudged to the cabinet and pulled out a pan, then opened the refrigerator and stared blankly at the shelves for a moment.

"Omelets," he mumbled finally. "Right."

* * *

Annie stepped back for a better look at herself in the full-length mirror on the back of her bedroom door. She was wearing a new red silk blouse with long sleeves gathered on narrow wristbands and a full, navy-and-red paisley print skirt. On her feet were navy sandals with narrow, high heels. A silver cross lay in the opening of her blouse. Silver hoops dangled from her ears.

She had applied makeup more lavishly than usual—even adding a rose blush to her cheeks. The blush now seemed redundant, since her skin felt flushed all over. Heavens, why was she so nervous? She felt like a fifteen-year-old getting ready for her first date.

A rump roast and scalloped potatoes were baking in the oven. Rising yeast rolls sat on the kitchen counter ready to be popped into the oven at the proper time. Waiting in the refrigerator were a crunchy Waldorf salad and chocolate mousse in tall, slender crystal glasses. Sam was coming to dinner.

It wasn't Sam's coming that had her nerves taut, Annie told herself as she went to check on the roast. It was the meal she had planned and prepared so carefully. Her talents were not in the kitchen. She didn't usually enjoy cooking—it wasn't much fun cooking for one, so she rarely did so. She got by on take-out food, frozen dinners, soup and sandwiches. But she'd invested a lot of time and energy in tonight's meal, and she wanted it to be perfect.

Ever since Sam had talked to her—really talked to her finally—about his childhood, a week ago, she'd had the feeling that their relationship was even more fragile than before. After that night, they both had drawn back a bit to reassess the situation. Annie thought Sam needed some time alone to come to terms with what he'd told her. She herself wanted to believe it was a breakthrough—putting into words one's pain and fear was supposed to be purging, wasn't it?—but she was afraid of expecting too much.

When she answered Sam's knock, he strode into the apartment hastily, with Callie draped over his shoulder. He deposited the squirming dog on the living-room carpet. Callie immediately began running around the apartment, sniffing in corners.

"I could get good at this," Sam announced, his eyes drinking her in hungrily. "I slunk past your landlord's apartment as silently as a cat burglar."

"I'm impressed." Annie returned his grin.

"Carrying that dog is like toting a load of bricks," he complained, brushing at dog hairs on his jacket.

"I'm glad you brought her," Annie said. "I'm delighted to have her here, even if it is for only a few hours."

He walked over to her slowly. His arms encircled her. "Are you delighted to have me?"

Annie tilted her head to one side and lifted her chin. With a teasing twinkle in her eyes, she gave him a quick kiss. "Deeply, but don't let it go to your head."

When she would have stepped back, he wrapped his arms around her waist and pulled her close. "*You* go to my head."

Annie gave him another light kiss, lingering a fraction longer this time. "The roast—" she began. The rest of the sentence was smothered by his lips.

The kiss was long, deep, infinitely savoring and smoldering with passion. Annie felt the weakness of desire stealing over her, turning her bones to jelly. His hands cradled her head, tilting it back to taste more deeply of her mouth. Clinging, Annie strained against him, inviting him to take more. For the moment she let herself be swept along by the sweet pleasure of being in Sam's embrace. But soon, she knew, kissing wouldn't be enough. Then dinner would be forgotten. The knowledge thrilled her, and she was tempted to let it happen. Still, she pulled away with a sigh, there was plenty of time.

"I've slaved over a hot stove all day," she said lightly. "You are going to be so proud of me." She spun away from him and started toward the kitchen. "Would you like to pour the wine, Sam?"

Callie met them, carrying a damp towel in her mouth and her tail wagging furiously. She wanted to play Fetch.

"Drop it," Annie ordered, and the dog obeyed instantly. "I've been so busy since I got home from work I haven't had time to pick up around here," she added to Sam apologetically while bending to snatch up the towel.

As soon as her face was within licking reach, Callie kissed her cheek. Laughing, Annie embraced the dog. "What a ham," she said, rumpling the dog's soft, droopy ears. "I can't play with you now, girl. Later."

Watching her with Callie, Sam admitted to himself how lonely his neat, orderly house had become and how empty his life was without Annie. He loved her. He thought it likely that he always would, and that was scary.

Sam had spent his life learning to be dependent on no one. But he needed Annie. He wanted a lifetime with her, and he couldn't be happy with less. Still, he wasn't ready to tell Annie that. He wasn't yet confident that it would be received this time any better than it had been before. She had walked out on him once; she could do it again.

Leaving Callie, Annie washed her hands at the sink and put the rolls in the oven. The table in the kitchen alcove was spread with a linen cloth and set for two. Sam popped the cork on a bottle of wine and filled the wineglasses.

Annie talked about her day as she worked. Sam only half attended. He was watching her bright-colored skirt swirl around her slender legs as she moved about the kitchen, producing a discernible tightening in his loins. He dragged his gaze away and responded with a few details of his own day. It was the sort of rehashing of the day's events that Annie needed, he told himself. Even if he was perfectly content to look at and listen to her in silence, he had vowed to try to change.

When they sat down at the table, Annie waited expectantly for his reaction to the meal while pretending to be intent on buttering a roll.

Sam ate without speaking for a few seconds, aware of her alertness. He understood and smiled to himself. "The roast is cooked just the way I like it."

Annie's eyes lit up.

"And these rolls," Sam continued expansively, "melt in your mouth."

Annie flushed with pleasure. "I made them from scratch."

Sam shook his head. "Don't ever try to tell me again that you can't cook."

Satisfied, Annie took up knife and fork to cut her meat. "It's the time cooking requires, I guess. I'm usually late getting home from work, and it's easier to put a frozen dinner in the microwave."

Sam had heard that faint discouragement in her voice before when she'd spoken of her work. "You work mighty hard at a job you don't seem too happy with," he observed.

Annie chewed thoughtfully for a moment. Sam was right. In the beginning the extra hours had seemed justified, the way to advancement. And work had kept her mind off Sam. When she'd been motivated by such strong goals, she hadn't minded overtime. She had welcomed it.

"I enjoyed my job at first," she said. "Harry Layman made a lot of promises about the future. Fast advancement, more responsibility, more money. In all fairness, he had no idea the state's depressed economy would continue for so long. He's probably too worried about his own future now to think about mine. But I'm awfully tired of broken promises." She didn't add that work no longer kept her mind off Sam. She thought about him all the time these days.

"Why don't you find another job?"

"I've considered it," Annie admitted. "Lately, I've been thinking about it a lot. I'm about ready to mail out some résumés." She took a bite of salad and buttered another roll.

Sam lifted his glass, studying her over the rim. Now was the time to mention the plan that had been taking form in his mind.

"Have you made any progress with finding an agent for Callie?" Annie asked.

"Not yet."

Her eyes darted to his in surprise. "Sam, we'll be free of Barnes in less than three weeks. Don't you think you should be looking a little harder?"

"I've talked to several people in the business," he said offhandedly. "I've also corresponded with two agents."

"And?"

"I wasn't real impressed with either of them. I have somebody else in mind."

"Who?"

He looked at her for a long moment before he said, "You."

Annie almost choked on her wine. "That's crazy," she sputtered, sloshing wine on the cloth as she set her glass down. "I don't know anything about that business."

"You're an intelligent woman. You can learn. I think you'd probably enjoy it."

"That's hardly the point."

He shrugged off her objections. "The commission and your half of the remainder of the earnings wouldn't come to as much as you're making now, but the potential for more is there. You could probably keep your job at the savings and loan for a while and do this on the side."

Good Lord, Annie thought, he's serious. He's thought this through. "What potential, Sam? Heavens, I wouldn't even know where to start."

"Just listen to me for a minute, Annie," Sam said a bit impatiently. "I didn't know anything either until I started talking to people in the business. Right now animals are big in TV commercials. Nothing sells like kids and animals. Did you know they even have Canine Oscars? And some dog food company is staging a national beauty contest for dogs. One agency representative told me that they get as many as five hundred calls for animals weekly from ad agencies and directors."

"That has to be a big agency," Annie put in. "They probably represent hundreds of animals."

"But they had to start small," Sam persisted. "I'm not suggesting that you search out other animals to represent, not now, anyway. But I do think we could do a lot more with Callie. The contract with the dog food company stipulates that she can't be used to represent any other dog food company in any commercial medium during the term of her contract with them. It says nothing about other types of companies—or animal organizations like the SPCA."

Still astonished by what he was suggesting, Annie asked, "What makes you think *I* could do as good a job as somebody who's already in the business?"

"Because you love Callie and she'd be your sole client, to start with, anyway. You'd have her best interests at heart."

Well, that was true. But was it enough? "Oh, Sam, I don't know...."

"Just think about it. That's all I'm asking."

She laughed, excited by the idea in spite of herself. "I'll give it some thought. But you have to promise me that if I decide I can't do it, you won't try to change my mind."

"Done."

They said no more about the subject during meal, but Annie's thoughts kept returning to it. She had to admit that it would be fun to learn all the ins and outs of representing Callie. If it turned out she could afford to do it full-time, she could accompany Callie to L.A. for tapings and stay on for a few days to make contact with other people working in the business.

Once she felt confident with what she was doing, she could find other animal clients. She might buy another dog herself, a different breed—and maybe a couple of cats. It would be like her childhood years when there were always several animals around. She'd have to find another place to live, but that was a minor detail.

It would be a challenge and Annie did her best work when she was challenged.

Whenever Annie was silent for any length of time, Sam knew she was thinking deeply about something. His suggestion had intrigued her, he could tell. He was pleased with himself. In a few days, when he was sure she was hooked, he'd spring the rest of his plan on her.

By the time they finished dinner, Callie was begging to go outside. "She won't give us any peace until we take her for a walk," Annie said.

Sam had something else in mind. "It's going to rain," he said. As if to confirm his words, thunder rumbled distantly. He looked at the ceiling and said piously, "Thank you, Lord."

Annie tried to keep a sober face, but her eyes danced. "We'll take an umbrella."

Callie cocked her head at Sam and barked.

"Ah, she's begging," Annie said. "Surely you can't refuse when she's asking so nicely."

Sam groaned as Annie pulled him from his chair. "Okay, I know when I'm outnumbered."

A fine mist was falling as they left the apartment. Annie held Callie's leash and Sam took the umbrella, his other arm around Annie's waist to keep her close. Once they were clear of the apartment complex, they strolled slowly, much to Callie's disgust. Since she couldn't run, the dog contented herself with dashing back and forth from bush to tree to flower bed in front of them.

Thunder cracked, sounding nearer than before, and Annie instinctively leaned closer to Sam. Her scent teased his nostrils. He halted and turned her to him, keeping the umbrella over them.

Annie looked up at him with a slow smile. Along with Sam's scent she smelled the fragrance of damp leaves and grass. There was no sound of other footsteps, no passing cars in the street. The night and the drizzling rain enclosed them in a magical, surreal world of scent and the soft sound of lightly falling rain.

"I love walking in the rain with you," Annie murmured. "I don't think we've ever done it before."

"You're beautiful," Sam said.

Callie was tugging impatiently on the leash, forgotten. Suddenly Annie felt special, blessed. "No, I'm not," she protested.

"To me you are," Sam said as his eyes roamed her face.

The fine rain was blowing in on them, washing Annie's face. She smiled up at Sam, blinking raindrops from her lashes. "We're getting wet."

"So we are." He kissed her. The taste of rain was on her lips. He lingered over the kiss. Callie gave up tugging and sat down at their feet. "Your face is wet." His lips brushed her brow, pausing at the hairline. "Your lashes are stuck together and your eyes are shining. Are you sure you aren't some otherworldly creature who's drifted out of the mist?"

Annie was too moved by the uncharacteristic imagery to speak. Instead she shook her head. A quick throb of need for him surged through her, and she shivered.

Sam shook off the spell spun by the mist and Annie's lovely, smiling face. "You're chilled. Let's go back." He gripped her arm and reversed their direction, their pace quicker than before.

Callie followed along obediently. "I think she's out of the mood for a walk," Annie said.

"We'll give her a bowl of milk, divert her attention."

"Divert her attention from what?"

Sam winked wickedly. "From us. We'll be otherwise occupied."

"I see," she said, wanting him with every fiber of her being.

They reached the apartment. Callie proceeded to shake the water out of her coat, spraying their legs. Simultaneously they stepped out of range, bumping into each other. Sam steadied her, then took the opportunity to kiss her lingeringly.

"Let's get inside where it's dry," Annie said breathlessly. Sam took her key and opened the door. In the darkened living room, he caught Annie to him again and captured her lips in another long, quiet kiss.

"Sam," she whispered, her blood singing with excitement and desire. "I want you."

For a moment they clung tightly to each other. "Wait here," Sam said. "I'll get Callie some milk and shut her in the kitchen." He released her. She heard him speak to Callie in the kitchen and open the refrigerator door. Annie shivered and, folding her arms, ran her hands up and down her sleeves.

Then Sam was back, reaching for her, his mouth finding hers in the darkness. They didn't turn on a light. They fumbled with damp clothing in the dark, stopping to kiss, fumble with more buttons, and kiss again. All the while, they were moving across the living room, leaving a trail of damp clothing on the way to Annie's bed.

Nine

I scares me sometimes—how much I need you," Sam whispered, his lips against her brow.

They lay in the tranquil aftermath of loving. The bedroom windows admitted the faint light of the street lamp, creating eerie shadows in the room. The dresser and armoire were hazy smudges against the wall.

When Annie didn't reply, Sam asked, "You do *know* how much I need you, don't you?"

"I know that you need me physically," Annie murmured.

"Oh, yes," he conceded, "but I'm talking about needing *you*, not just your body."

Annie stirred a bit restlessly. She turned on her back. They lay side by side, only their hands touching. "I'm afraid, Sam."

"Welcome to the club."

"I just find it hard to believe that you need me as deeply as you think you do. You don't really need anyone."

The words hung between them, echoes from the past. Sam tried to ignore his own wounded feelings and focus on Annie's. If he'd done that before, she might not have left him. "I never wanted to need people," he said quietly. "I worked hard at it."

"I know," Annie sighed. Her fingers tightened in his. "That's what finally defeated me when we were together before. I just couldn't deal with it anymore, Sam."

Wordlessly he gathered her in his arms, holding her tightly and burying his face in her hair, breathing in her sweet, familiar scent. Her arms tightened convulsively around his midsection, and her breath was warm against his neck. Her breathing was ragged, and he knew that she was fighting tears. He stroked her shoulder and back, seeking to comfort her and perhaps comfort himself, as well. He held her quietly, unable to speak.

He had always been too concerned with his own vulnerability to worry much about Annie's. She'd seemed so strong to him, so resilient. There were no deep, psychic wounds in her childhood. She had grown up protected, sheltered, valued—secure in the unfailing love of both her parents. Sam couldn't even imagine what such a childhood would be like.

Maybe growing up as Annie had didn't make one less vulnerable, after all. Somehow she remained convinced that he didn't need her as much as she needed him, when to Sam it seemed the reverse was true.

Love and need. To Annie they were different things. Was it possible that she had gone on loving him, even when she left him? Was it possible that she had never stopped? In the past few weeks they had talked of wants and needs, but the word "love" had not passed between them.

Even love hadn't been enough before. Could they learn to understand each other better this time, so that he wouldn't lose her again?

Her arms around him relaxed as her breathing turned slow and even.

"Annie?"

She didn't answer. She was asleep.

Sam lay awake, his hands moving gently over the silky warmth of her skin, caressing, cherishing, comforted by the weight of her head on his shoulder, her arm across his chest.

All the next week Annie thought about Sam's suggestion that she become Callie's agent. She looked at it from every possible angle. The more she thought about it, the more intrigued she was by the challenge, the opportunity to start a new career.

She had roughed out a new budget. If she quit her job, her income from commissions and her half of the owners' royalties should be enough for her to scrape by on—barely, if she lived frugally. And she had saved some money while working at the savings and loan, so she'd have a cushion for emergencies.

She'd have to work out of her home, and she'd like to have a place with a yard for Callie and room for other animals eventually, if she decided to expand. She might someday operate a kennel and breed registered dogs for additional income.

But more space meant more rent, and she didn't see how she could fit it into the lean budget she'd prepared.

The sensible thing to do, she knew, was to keep her job at the savings and loan for a while. She could schedule her vacation for the last half of June and take Callie to L.A. for the next taping. In the meantime she could work with Callie evenings and weekends. It didn't leave much time for learning the intricacies of the agenting business, but it just might work for the time being.

She wasn't completely happy with this scenario. These days she dreaded going to her office, but this wasn't the time to look for another job, not if her attention and interest were going to be focused on representing Callie.

She decided to take a few more days to think it over.

Sam phoned Friday morning before she left for work. She had been out to see Callie twice since they'd had dinner at her apartment, but Sam hadn't been home either time.

Sam's secretary had called her Wednesday to tell her that Sam had been called out of town unexpectedly and he'd wanted Annie to know. The message pleased Annie. It showed that Sam was sensitive to Annie's need to be kept apprised of his comings and goings. He really was trying to change.

"I got back to town late last night," Sam said now. "I wanted to call you, but I knew you'd be asleep. I missed you, Annie. It seems like it's been a year since I saw you."

"Four days," Annie said, smiling, "and it does seem like a year. By the way, thank you for having your secretary phone me."

"You liked that, did you?"

"Very much."

"Ah...if only you were here so I could kiss you, woman. Maybe I should swing by the savings and loan and take care of that little item on my way to the office."

"That would be lovely," Annie mused, "but I don't think my boss would be pleased."

"He's not a romantic, I take it."

"Hardly."

"Well, I guess I can wait for a few more hours. Can you come out to my place this evening?"

"Are you going to cook for me?"

"If that's what it takes to get you here. What would you like to eat?"

"Why don't you surprise me?"

"All right. I'll try to be home by six, so come as early as you want. I have something I want to show you."

"What?"

"I can't describe it on the telephone. You have to see it to appreciate it." His voice took on a teasing note. "I promise you won't be disappointed."

"Uh-huh. Is this an obscene phone call, Bennington?"

He laughed. "Now that you mention it, honey, I could get into that."

"I have to go to work," Annie said, "but hold the thought. Save it for later."

"Oh, I will," Sam assured her.

Annie thought five o'clock would never arrive. She worked straight through her lunch hour and took no coffee breaks, trying to get as much of the work on her desk completed as possible before leaving for the day.

Layman called to her from his office as Annie was leaving. "Where are you going so early?"

"It's five o'clock," Annie said.

"When did you turn into a clock-watcher?" Layman inquired, checking his wristwatch—to see if she was lying, Annie assumed.

"I have an appointment this evening, Harry. See you tomorrow." Ignoring his disapproving scowl, Annie hurried out of the savings and loan.

Her habit of coming to work early and staying late may have been a mistake, Annie thought dryly as she got into her car. All it seemed to have accomplished was to make her boss think she was shirking when she left at five like everyone else.

As she drove out of the parking lot and turned her car in the direction of her apartment, Annie realized she'd forgotten to put her name on the vacation schedule for the last half of June. She must remember to do it tomorrow. She didn't think anybody else was scheduled for that time, but Layman liked to be informed about vacations well in advance.

Before heading for Sam's, Annie showered and dressed in a simple, jade-green cotton dress with bands of white lace down the bodice. Her feet were bare in white sandals. Using her brush lightly, she coaxed her curls into soft disorder around her face. Then she spun around in front of the full-length mirror, examining herself critically.

"I wish I had bigger boobs," she muttered aloud. Fortunately, Sam seemed perfectly happy with her boobs the way they were. Smiling, she grabbed her purse and left the apartment.

Sam must have been looking for her car, for he opened the door the instant her finger touched the bell. He looked lean and fit in low-riding jeans and a body-hugging white knit shirt. He reached for Annie and pulled her into the foyer. "You're late," he growled as he spun her into his arms.

She looked up at him, her eyes bright with happiness. "It's not even six-thirty."

His mouth lowered to brush tantalizingly against hers. "I expected you at six." He nibbled provocatively at the corner of her mouth. "I've been walking the floor for half an hour. You taste wonderful, Annie."

She wanted badly to succumb at once to the invitation in his husky voice, and in his eyes when he drew back to look down at her. Her gaze strayed to his mouth, which offered such delights. But she needed just to be with him for a while first, to savor his presence at dinner, to talk to him about becoming Callie's agent.

"I've been dying all day to see what you have to show me," Annie said.

He brushed his fingers through her hair. "You always did have more than your share of curiosity."

"You deliberately piqued my curiosity with that phone call this morning, Sam Bennington," Annie accused. "Now you have the audacity to criticize me."

"It wasn't a criticism, pet." He lifted her chin with fingers and studied her mouth. When his eyes lifted to meet hers, they glinted with a depth of feeling that made Annie tremble. "Close your eyes, Annie."

Her eyes clung to his for a moment before she complied. Gently his mouth lowered to hers, and his arms tightened as the kiss grew lengthy and intimate. "What were you saying, sweet?" he murmured as he changed the angle of the kiss.

Annie gathered her scattered thoughts. "You were going to show me something," she reminded him, her voice unsteady.

"So I was." He sighed and lifted his head. "You remember what curiosity did to the cat, don't you?"

"Sam—" she began warningly.

"Keep your eyes closed."

"What—?"

He dropped his arms and took her hand. "Just do it, and don't look until I say."

Annie closed her eyes. Sam led her through the house, glancing back to make certain she wasn't peeking. When he halted, he said, "Okay, you can look now."

Annie's eyes flew open. They stood in an oak paneled room that smelled of paint and varnish. Bookshelves lined one wall, and the floor was covered with deep blue carpeting. At the windows were plantation shutters stained with the same golden color as the paneling.

Annie whirled around, taking in the room. It was one of the rooms that Sam had been working on the past few weeks. The last time she'd looked in here there had been no paneling, no carpeting, no bookshelves.

"I don't need four bedrooms," Sam said, "so I decided to turn it into an office."

"It's beautiful!" Annie exclaimed. "When did you have time to do all this?"

"I hired a contractor to finish it. I talked him into working this in ahead of other jobs. I told him I needed it right away."

Annie looked at him quizzically. "Are you going to start working at home more?"

"It's not for me, Annie. It's for you."

She looked bewildered.

"If you decide to be Callie's agent, you'll need an office," Sam explained. "There's a desk and file cabinet at the firm that nobody's using. I could move them in here."

"Oh, Sam!" With a delighted laugh, Annie threw her arms around his neck. "I *have* been thinking about it, almost constantly since you mentioned it. I probably should keep my job at the savings and loan for the time being, but if this goes well . . . what I mean is, I'd really like to try it."

He gave her a self-satisfied grin. "I'll have the desk and file cabinet moved Monday and I'll have a house key made for you, too, so you can come and go at will. You'll also need a phone. By Tuesday you'll be in business."

Working out of Sam's house, where Callie was, sounded ideal, but Annie was not unaware of the problems it could cause. "I'll keep out of your way when I'm working here," she said. "This has to be separate, Sam. This is business and the other—" she hesitated, not knowing how to describe the still fragile relationship that was developing between them "—that's something else entirely."

Sam noted her hesitation and would have given much to know what passed through her mind in that moment. He nodded, thinking that she still had reservations about him, about the relationship.

Annie walked around the room, trying to decide where to put the desk and file cabinet. Sam watched her absorption for a moment, then said, "I'll go check on dinner."

Annie glanced at him distractedly. "I'll be with you in a few minutes."

Sam left her and went to the kitchen. Once she was alone, Annie let the misgivings she had been holding at bay trickle into her mind. Things were moving too fast. What if it didn't work out with Sam? What if it did? As long as she was employed at the savings and loan, she would have to work with Callie evenings and weekends—when Sam was home.

It was one thing to go to Sam's place for dinner, but quite another to have a key to his house and come and go at odd hours. But knowing he was in the house would be distracting if she was trying to work. Even if he wasn't home, how could she keep her business relationship with him separated from their personal life? She would be here in this house that bore his handiwork everywhere she turned, where his scent lingered in every room.

The truth was that Annie couldn't forget that Sam had said nothing about love. He had claimed that he needed her, but was that enough? Sam had worked out an elaborate system of self-protection, and he had a will of iron. She suspected that he could no longer trust her enough to admit the depth of his feelings, as he once had.

She had hurt him terribly when she'd left him. At the time she'd been too involved with her own pain to think about his. But she was wiser now. The things he had told her about his childhood helped her to better understand why Sam was the man he was, though that didn't make Sam's defense mechanisms any easier to deal with. Nor did it make her own need for intimacy on all levels any less real.

Her misgivings stayed at the back of her mind during dinner, a Mexican dish oozing with cheese and spices.

"You're awfully quiet," Sam observed as they left the table.

"I'm just thinking about what I'm taking on as Callie's agent, all the things I have to learn, the contacts I need to make in the next few weeks." She walked to the French doors and smiled at Callie, who sat on the deck watching them. "Tomorrow I'll put in for vacation time during the last half of June so I can take Callie to L.A. for the tapings." She heard Sam behind her but didn't turn. "There's so much to do in such a short time."

Sam sensed a tenseness in her, and he wondered if it was entirely due to the business with Callie. When he'd shown her the office, she'd seemed to withdraw from him a little. Had he assumed too much? Maybe he shouldn't have sprung the office on her without warning.

Was she worried because the office was here in his house? Did she think he was trying to take over her life, push her into making a commitment before she was ready? Hell, would she ever be ready?

It occurred to Sam that he'd confessed his need for her on several occasions, providing a perfect opportunity for her to confess her own feelings. In the past she'd talked about them at length. She was more cautious now, though, and that made Sam feel sad; he knew that he had caused Annie's new restraint, the diminishment of her natural spontaneity, which he had always found so delightful.

Once she had loved him without reservation. She had told him so with great frequency. He tried to convince himself that they were moving slowly back to what they once had together. But she hadn't said she loved him yet, and he sensed a gap between them. He was still unsure of what lay ahead for them.

He thought that, in spite of his best efforts to make things right, he could drive her away again. He studied her, calculating how to bridge the gap before it grew wider.

He placed his hands on her shoulders and felt a tremor pass through her. She bowed her head, and he took the opportunity to kiss the nape of her neck.

She made a little sound of surrender and turned into his arms. "I thought you were never going to touch me," she whispered. Her eyes were huge and vulnerable.

He gave her a quiet, measuring look. "I was waiting for some indication that you wanted me to."

Annie couldn't read his thoughts. He was protecting them from her. Nerves began to jump in her stomach. "The mere fact that I'm here should be indication enough."

He scanned her face in silence for a moment. "Maybe it should be. I'm not reading you very well these days. Tell me what you're thinking about right now."

A tremulous smile tugged at her lips. "I'm wondering why we're wasting time on this inane conversation when we could be making love."

She lifted a hand to his cheek, and he felt the tension inside him beginning to uncurl. Whatever else went wrong, she was still eager for him. He pressed his hand over hers as it brushed his cheek. Holding her eyes with his, he turned her hand over and brought his mouth to the palm. Gentleness lifted the shades from his eyes as he looked at her.

"I've lain awake every night since the last time we were together, aching for you," he muttered. He tilted her head back and kissed her with great tenderness. "You're in my blood, sweet Annie," he told her as his hand caressed the warm length of her back.

"Sam." Annie wrapped her arms around him and burrowed her face into his neck. At last her misgivings were stealing away, leaving only her love and desire for him. "You make me tremble."

"Ah, Annie, I'm going to give you such pleasure." This time his kiss was long and lingering. Annie's bones melted instantly. Her mouth clung to his, sweet and hungry, and his quiet moan of pleasure rumbled in his throat.

"Not on the carpet," she murmured breathlessly against his mouth. "My skin's still tender from last time."

"I'll rub you with soothing lotion—everywhere," he promised as he came back to her mouth.

"That sounds lovely," Annie said, drawing away enough to smile at him dreamily. "I'll think of something equally wonderful to do to you."

His eyes were lit with growing desire. "I can't wait," he said huskily. He kissed her, his mouth more possessively greedy this time. Then, lifting her in his arms, he started toward the bedroom.

The doorbell chimed, intruding on Annie's dreamy, floating mood. Sam cursed and his steps slowed. "Who could that be?" Annie murmured against his neck.

"I have a pretty good idea," Sam muttered as the doorbell chimed again. "If we ignore him, maybe he'll go away."

Before the chimes died away, the caller began pounding on the door and calling Sam's name. Annie sighed. "Sounds like Jude Preston. I don't think he's going anywhere, do you?"

"Damn." Sam set her on her feet, giving her a quick, hot kiss before answering the door.

Annie followed Sam through the living room, stopping when she could see into the foyer. Jude Preston stepped inside, his eyes going past Sam to alight on Annie.

"Sorry to disturb you, Sam," he said, grinning a bit foolishly, "but I'm in a bad fix. My water pump's gone out on me and there's not a drop of water in the house."

"Take all the water you need, Jude," Sam said. "You can use the faucet in front."

Preston scratched his head. "I need to get the problem fixed tonight. Got a little job to do for a fellow a mile south, starting early tomorrow morning.

Probably take three or four days, and I can use the money. The pump's waterlogged. Happened once before. I can fix it in an hour or two. But I'll háve to pull the pump, and I can't do it by myself. I thought maybe you could help me, Sam."

Sam threw Annie an unhappy look. "Sure, Jude. I'll be over in a minute."

"Sure 'preciate it, Sam."

Sam closed the door and dragged a hand through his hair. "I knew I shouldn't have answered the door."

"He knew we were in here," Annie pointed out. "Our cars are in the drive."

"Yeah." He went to her. "I'm sorry, sweetheart." His hands settled at her waist.

She lifted her shoulders. "It's all right—well, not all right—but it can't be helped. He's been so good to look after Callie when you're gone. You have to go and help him." Her eyes reflected the disappointment and regret that Sam was feeling.

He drew her against him and his lips roamed over her face before settling on her mouth. A few seconds later he lifted his head with reluctance. "You'll stay. I'll get back as soon as I can."

"No. I think I'd better go home. You could be gone for hours."

Sam nodded, not wanting her to go but knowing she was right. This wasn't the first time Preston had called on him for help in such a matter. Past experience had taught him that Jude's two-hour jobs often took much longer. "All right. We'll talk tomorrow." His mouth returned to hers for a brief moment, and then he was gone.

Annie expelled an unhappy sigh, her lovely evening with Sam destroyed by a waterlogged pump.

The next morning Annie learned that the alteration in her plans for the evening with Sam was not the only sudden change she had to deal with.

She arrived at work her usual half hour early. As soon as she had stashed her purse in a desk drawer and put the coffee on, she knocked on Layman's office door.

"Harry, can I talk to you for a sec?"

"Come on in."

Layman was hunched over an open file on his desk. As Annie approached the desk, she saw the name Dunwiller on the folder tab.

"Have you heard from Dunwiller since he stormed in here and read us all the riot act?" Annie inquired.

Layman looked up, a frown etched in his forehead. "Not a peep."

Annie turned a chair to face the desk and sat down. "You probably won't, either. He accomplished what he came here for—to get us off his back."

Layman closed the file and leaned back in his chair. "I'm going to let it ride for a while longer."

Annie knew Harry was hoping Dunwiller would come through with the back payments without his having to get involved. She didn't think it was going to happen. Furthermore, this preferential treatment irked her. "About twenty of our mortgage accounts have been in arrears this year and none of those loans is for more than seventy-five thousand."

"What's that got to do with this?"

"You were on my case about every last one of them as soon as they were thirty days past due. We don't let it ride when it's some working man barely making it from one paycheck to the next. Why should Dunwiller be any different?"

Layman made a sound of contempt. "Those poor working stiffs can't make my life uncomfortable."

Annie wanted to say that Layman's discomfort shouldn't be taken into consideration. But it wasn't the time to get into an argument with him. She'd come to ask him to put her vacation on the schedule.

"I'm just glad Dunwiller's account is your baby now."

He looked at her as if to say she'd catch her share of the grief if it came to that. "I've finally decided when I want my vacation," Annie said. "I'd like you to add it to the schedule."

Layman opened his bottom desk drawer, shuffled through folders and drew out the one containing the vacation list. He reached for a pen. "Give me the dates."

"June fourteen through the end of the month. I'll still have another week coming, but I'll save it for later."

Layman studied the schedule, pen poised. "The regional S and L conference is scheduled for the week of the fourteenth in Dallas."

Annie had forgotten that, but she didn't see it as a reason to change her plans. "I know you don't like me to be gone when you are, but I'll get everything caught up before I leave. The secretaries can handle anything that comes up until you get back."

He shook his head. "I was planning to send you this year. My kid's scheduled for knee surgery that week. He injured it playing T-ball. They're going to repair some cartilage and put on a cast."

"Harry, it's imperative that I get my vacation at that time. I have to take care of some personal business." She knew better than to say the business had to do with her dog. Although she had told Layman about Callie's contract with the dog food company, he refused to take it seriously.

His face was getting red. It infuriated Layman when an employee questioned his decisions. "Whatever it is, it'll have to wait. I want you in Dallas the week of the fourteenth."

Annie kept her voice calm and reasonable. "Could you just give me a break here? Very little is accomplished at those conferences, anyway, except for some record hangovers."

Layman stared at her as he rose slowly to his feet. "This is not open to discussion."

Annie stood, too. "Harry, I've always suited my vacations to your plans before. I work hard around here, and this is the first time I've ever asked you to give in on a point for my convenience. You know as well as I do that neither one of us has to be in Dallas."

"I happen to disagree with you. The subject is closed. Please shut the door when you leave."

Annie was so angry she could hardly speak. She clenched her hands together and struggled to gain control of her composure. Then she said, "I'm sorry you feel that way, Harry. You don't leave me any alternative. I quit."

Harry gaped at her as though stupefied. *"What?"*

"I no longer work for you, Harry. I'll go and clear out my desk. I'll be back in half an hour for my paycheck. Don't forget to include the four weeks of vacation time I have coming."

Annie spun on her heel and walked out. By the time she reached her office, she was shaking with reaction.

Layman followed her. "Are you serious? You're going to quit just because I want you to put off your vacation for one week?"

"This is merely the last straw," said Annie wearily. "It's been coming for a long time."

Furious, Layman glared at her another moment and left, mumbling something about it being her funeral.

Annie wondered if he was right. Slowly her anger was being replaced by anxiety. Dear God, what had she done? She sat down at her desk and buried her face in her hands. Just calm down, she told herself, it's not the end of the world. You hated the job, anyway.

Finally she lifted her head and took a deep, bracing breath. She'd have plenty of time to devote to developing her fledgling agency now. Maybe this was a blessing in disguise.

But she would be without a regular, dependable paycheck. It felt more like a disaster than a blessing.

Ten

Annie began her workday in the new office at Sam's house later than she had at the savings and loan. She arrived about nine-thirty and left before five, making it a point to reach Sam's after he left for the city and to be gone before he got home.

It was Sam's house, not hers. She had promised herself that she would keep the job and her personal relationship with Sam in totally separate compartments of her life.

She had given herself three months to come up with a plan to increase Callie's income. If nothing had developed by then, she'd have to begin looking for another job.

In the meantime she was writing letters and making phone calls to introduce herself and Callie to any person or organization that might conceivably have need of an animal "star." Once she'd explained to the people in the marketing department at the Chow Hound company what she was doing and assured them that she wouldn't take on anything that would create a conflict of interest, they were extremely helpful. They provided her with ideas and leads and scheduled two full days for her to spend conferring with their marketing manager in mid-July.

They had suggested that she concentrate on local organizations at first, and Annie thought that good advice. In her first two weeks on the job, she met with representatives of Animal Aid, SPCA, pet stores and an animal health supply company headquartered in Oklahoma City. All of them were interested to learn that the famous Chow Hound dog was now an Oklahoma resident, and Annie had reason to hope that an occasional job would come from these meetings.

By letter, she contacted similar organizations in cities within a few hours' drive of Oklahoma City, enclosing her new business card and several eight-by-ten color photos of Callie taken by a professional photographer who had come out to the house.

She made arrangements for the trip to L.A., reserving a room in a hotel that allowed animal guests and adjoined a park where she and Callie could get their daily exercise. And she spent more time working with Callie, slowly adding new commands to those the dog understood and reacted to.

She managed to keep occupied, but no matter how busy she was, her mind continued to stray to Sam at odd, unexpected moments. They had been together three times in the past two weeks. Their lovemaking served as a catharsis, but the release from tension was only temporary.

When they weren't making love, there was a feeling of walking on eggshells about their relationship. Annie knew they couldn't go on that way indefinitely. She was going to have to talk to Sam about the doubts and fears that churned inside her. *But not yet,* she told herself as she signed the last of a stack of letters. *Wait until I know if this agenting business is going to work out. I can't deal with everything at once.*

She folded the letter and sealed the envelope. Was she being a coward? Maybe. Still, she needed a little more time to think through exactly what she wanted from Sam before she confronted him about what he was willing to give. Sighing, she began to add stamps to envelopes just as the doorbell rang.

Callie barked and ran ahead of Annie to the door. "You sound ferocious," Annie told her, "but we know you wouldn't hurt a fly."

Annie peeked through the glass and saw Jude Preston standing on the porch with his dog, Bud. Annie hadn't seen him since the night he'd come to get Sam's help with his water pump.

She opened the door. "Hi, Jude."

"You busy, Annie?"

"I'm just winding things up for today."

"Sam told me how hard you been working, getting Callie some jobs."

"Afraid I haven't gotten her any yet. I'm still putting out feelers."

He shifted from one foot to the other and jingled the change in his overalls pocket. Annie sensed he had something to say to her, but didn't quite know how.

"There's still some coffee in the pot. Would you like to come in and have a cup?"

"Sure, that'd be great. Stay here, Bud." He followed Annie into the kitchen. "I'd kind of like to talk to you about something—a business proposition."

Annie turned on the burner under the coffeepot and took down two mugs. "Oh?"

He straddled a kitchen chair and wrapped his arms around the chair back. "It's about Bud." He waited, as though expecting some response from her.

"Yes?"

"Well, I got to thinking, seeing as how you're getting in the business of finding work for Callie, you might hear of something old Bud could do on TV. He's naturally a smart dog, you know. And he minds real good."

He looked so hopeful that Annie hadn't the heart to tell him that she couldn't see Bud as a television star. "Well, uh, from what little I've learned so far, most ad agencies prefer female dogs. They're more docile, easier to work with."

"Bud's real easy to work with. 'Course, if you found him a job, I'd give him a bath and brush his coat, get him all spiffed up."

He was so sincere that Annie had to struggle not to smile. She was growing fond of Sam's neighbor. "I'll keep it in mind, Jude. But Callie's case is a bit different because she was already under contract when Sam and I got her."

"I understand. I just thought you could put Bud on your client list, or whatever you call it, and if you hear of anything, you could let me know."

"All right." The coffee was hot, so Annie filled the two mugs, handing one to Jude. As she sat down at the table she glanced at the clock on the wall. It was four-fifty, and she liked to be on the road by five.

Jude was in the mood to chat. He started a long, involved tale about his days as an oil-pipeline welder in Saudi Arabia. Annie murmured appropriate responses at intervals and tried to look interested, while sneaking surreptitious looks at her wristwatch. She couldn't bring herself to cut him off for fear of hurting his feelings.

Twenty minutes later, Jude rose to go. Annie accompanied him to the door. "I'll be seeing you," he said. "You'll call me if you hear of anything for Bud?"

"You bet," Annie assured him as she shut the door.

She hurried back to the office to pick up her purse and the letters that were ready for mailing. As she started out of the office, the telephone rang. She dropped her purse and the letters on the desk and grabbed the receiver.

"Annie Malloy's office."

"Miss Malloy, this is Bob Trayler over at Trayler's Pet Center."

The name was vaguely familiar. Trayler's name must be on the list she'd sent mailings to last week. "Yes, Mr. Trayler."

"The wife and I are putting in a second store in the new mall that's opening on July fourth."

"Spring Park." There had been a lot of coverage of the new mall in the local newspapers. Supposedly, it would be the largest mall in a four-state area.

"That's right. We got to talking after we received your letter and the pictures of California, and we took it up with the mall management. They're willing to go halves with us to bring California to the mall for the opening."

"Fantastic!"

"We'd like to have her there for two or three hours in the afternoon and another couple that evening, when we expect the most traffic. We thought we'd have a photographer there so kids could have their picture taken with her. What would the price tag be?"

Annie heard herself stating a sum that sounded too high when she said it aloud. She expected Trayler to try to bargain her down, but he didn't. "That sounds fine. If you can come into the store one day next week we'll work out the other details."

Annie was looking at the blank calendar page for the coming week. "How about Tuesday at two?"

"That sounds good. Talk to you then."

"Thank you for calling, Mr. Trayler." Annie dropped the receiver into the cradle and let out a squeal of delight. Callie trotted into the office, her ears perked up. Annie dropped to her knees and hugged the dog. "You've got a job, Callie! And he didn't bat an eye at the price!"

Callie wagged her tail and licked Annie's cheek, almost as if she understood what Annie had said. Annie uncapped a pen and noted her appointment with Trayler in next week's Tuesday square. As she was writing a note for Sam about the mall opening, she heard his car turning into the drive.

She looked at her watch and saw that it was five-thirty. Time had gotten away from her. Still, Sam was getting home earlier than usual.

A few moments later she heard his key in the lock. "Annie?"

She met him in the foyer. "Hi. I'm running late today, but Jude came by—he wants me to find Bud a TV job—and then I got a call from Bob Trayler—Trayler's Pet Center...."

She trailed off, noticing for the first time that he seemed to be only half listening. He looked tired and distracted. He tossed his briefcase in the hall closet and made a pass at her cheek with his mouth in passing. "I need a drink. Join me?"

She followed him into the dining room, watching as he made two mixed drinks. He handed her a glass. "You were saying?"

"Callie has a job. July fourth, for the opening of the new Spring Park Mall." Annie sipped her drink, thinking that she should have left before he got home. Did he think it presumptuous of her to still be there—as though she were waiting for him?

"Good. That's good," Sam murmured. He took a swallow of his drink and studied her thoroughly, carefully. He had not expected to find her there, but it was just as well that he had. He was going to have to talk, really talk, to her, with nothing held back. He had to know where he stood with her, even if the news was bad. He couldn't go on the way they had been, circling around each other like two wary animals, avoiding subjects that were likely to cause disagreements. These days he felt close to her only in bed. At other times, she often seemed a stranger to him.

Annie gazed at him, knowing that whatever he was thinking about was serious. His eyes were guarded but she had learned to recognize the signs that he had something heavy on his mind—the rigidity of his shoulders, the unnatural stillness.

She was suddenly afraid. She clutched her purse and the letters in one hand and set her drink down. Unlike Sam, when Annie was nervous she had to move. One of the many differences between them.

"I just remembered, I left two coffee mugs on the kitchen table." She fled to the kitchen, grabbed the mugs and washed them at the kitchen sink.

Sam followed her, drink in hand. She sensed his presence and turned to find him studying her. "I keep leaving things lying around. I'm sorry, Sam. I'll try to do better. I should keep all my clutter in my office."

"I don't expect you not to use the rest of the house." He frowned as she pulled open several drawers impatiently in search of a dish towel. She was uncomfortable in his presence. He downed the remainder of his drink and walked to the counter to set the glass down. "I didn't mean to sound disinterested in Callie's mall job. I think it's great. You're going to be a good agent. You have a way with people, Annie. I know you're going to increase the profits from Callie. I haven't been much support to you in getting this thing off the ground. I want to apologize."

"There's no need." Annie shook her head as she placed the dried mugs in the cabinet. "You've told me many times how demanding your job is. I didn't fully appreciate that in the past, but now I understand how hard it is to know where to draw the line when there's always more work than you can get done. You don't owe me an apology."

He took a step closer. In the other room, Callie scratched to be let out. "I thought my seeming lack of interest in what you're doing might have angered you. I'm trying to figure out what you're holding back, Annie."

"I don't even know where to begin," she said simply. Feeling a thickness rising in her throat, she spoke quickly. "I feel I have to consider every word before I say it. You know that doesn't come naturally to me. It's hard."

"I've sensed that, and I hate it," he countered. His eyes searched hers. "I always admired your spontaneity, maybe because of my natural reserve. We're so different."

"Too different, I sometimes think."

"I'm going to fix another drink," he said abruptly. Annie trailed after him to the dining room and picked up her own half-finished drink. Sam turned from the bar. In the living room, Callie scratched and whined.

"She wants out," Annie said, and moved toward the living room.

"Sit down," Sam said. "I'll tend to Callie."

Annie was too jumpy to sit. She stood beside the fireplace and sipped the drink. Sam closed the French doors behind Callie and faced her.

"I don't want to sit," she said apologetically. "You go ahead."

"No."

"Oh."

So they had come to this, Annie thought. Conversing in monosyllables. "I should go—"

"No," Sam said again. "Please."

Annie took a deep breath. "Sam, you look tired. I'll come back later, when you're rested."

He ignored the suggestion. "Tell me why you've changed, Annie."

She gave a quick laugh and brought her glass up to press against her forehead for an instant. "I'm scared."

"Of what?"

"Of saying the wrong thing—or saying the right thing in the wrong way." She lowered the glass and looked at him. "But you're right. I'm going to explode if I don't get it out. Perhaps I should start by saying I'm sorry. Maybe I asked too much of you before. Maybe I was naive, too idealistic. I wanted our relationship to be perfect, but nothing's ever perfect, is it?"

"Annie." He made a quick gesture of frustration. "It wasn't that I didn't *want* the same thing. It was just much harder for me to give myself."

"I understand that now. Oh, Sam, the problems weren't all your fault. I thought because you didn't show your feelings exactly as I did, that somehow they weren't as strong. It was unreasonable of me. If only you'd told me about your childhood sooner . . ."

"Would you have stayed with me if I had?"

"I don't know," she said honestly. She began to wander around the room. Standing still was no longer possible. "I wanted us to possess each other totally. Childish of me. But I did love you so very much, Sam."

Her use of the past tense was not lost on him. "We were both a bit unrealistic in our expectations, considering the people we were."

She moved her shoulders hopelessly. "And are, Sam?"

"I don't believe that people can't change." He drained his glass in a single swallow and deposited it on a lamp table. Then he stuffed his hands into his pants pockets. "I even talked to someone about it last week. A professional counselor."

She made a helpless gesture. "I—I think that could be beneficial, if you did it for yourself. Not if it was some kind of gesture for me."

"But it was for you, Annie. Don't you know you're the most important thing in my life?"

She stopped pacing to stare at him and shake her head.

"That was probably a stupid question." He walked to her, placed his hands on her shoulders. He rubbed the curve of her shoulders before dropping his hands. "I expected you to understand my feelings by osmosis, I guess. The truth is that a part of me couldn't quite believe you loved me as unreservedly as you said. I didn't feel worthy."

"Oh, Sam . . ."

He went on. "Holding back the words I knew you wanted was a way of protecting myself. There were many times when I was so full of loving you that I came close to breaking through the barrier. But the habits of a lifetime aren't easy to throw off, so when I was feeling particularly vulnerable, I stayed late at the office. It's only recently that I've worked all of this out in my mind. I couldn't see it at the time."

"Sam." Annie lifted a hand to his cheek. "You never had to protect yourself from me."

He brought her fingers to his lips, then let them go. "Let me finish, Annie. When you left me, it seemed to confirm the doubts I'd had all along. I told myself you'd never really loved me. I had to believe that. Otherwise, I'd have had to admit that I'd made you so unhappy, that in spite of your love, I'd driven you away."

Annie swallowed, not certain she could speak without crying. "Those first few months, I was so unhappy I thought I'd die."

"I *wished* I could." He rubbed the pad of his thumb gently over the side of her throat. "I came close to coming after you hundreds of times. What stopped me was the fear that you didn't care enough to be moved by anything I could say or do."

Annie felt the warmth of hope enveloping her. She lifted her arms. "I cared too much. That was the trouble. I—"

Before she could finish, Sam's mouth claimed hers. "Annie," he said at length, pressing her head into the hollow of his neck. "Stop running back and forth to town. There's no need. Give up your apartment and move in here with me."

She pressed against him, deeply moved by the urgency in his voice. He did need her. Nothing else could have moved him to reveal so much of himself.

"Annie, will you say something?" he muttered.

She laughed shakily. "Tell me what to say, Sam. I don't know anymore."

"Say yes." He held her away from him to look deeply into her eyes, as though he wished he could climb into her head and direct her thoughts. "Say you love me as much as I love you."

Annie's eyes filled, misting her vision. Smiling and crying at the same time, she managed, "Oh, yes! Tell me again that you love me, Sam."

"I love you, Annie." He rubbed his cheek against hers. "I will never love anyone else. Marry me."

When they were together before, they'd spoken of marriage in a general sense. Both had been a little wary of the subject, fearing that the other wasn't ready for the commitment.

Never until now had Sam asked her directly to marry him. She was almost afraid to accept. She had to let Sam do things in his own way, move at his own pace. She had to let Sam be Sam. She'd made the mistake once before of trying to force him into a mold of her own designing.

She wrapped her arms around his neck and pulled him close. "We could live together for a while first. You shouldn't take a step like that until you're sure you're ready."

"I've never been more sure of anything in my life." Their lips met once, then again...and again. His hands slid beneath her blouse to caress gently. "I don't want to just live with you. It's too easy for you to walk away."

"Oh, sweetheart," she whispered, floating in a daze caused by the sensual touch of his hands. "I won't walk away again. It would destroy me. It almost did before." She slipped her hand under the collar of his shirt, felt the taut warmth of muscle and skin beneath her palm. "I warn you, this time I'll stay and fight for you if I have to."

"I want you to be my wife," he insisted. "I want a marriage."

She smiled up at him as he lifted his face. "And children."

"Several," Sam agreed.

A scratching sound intruded. "I hear Callie at the door," Annie sighed. "She wants back in."

"She can wait," Sam decided, and lowered his mouth to hers. Annie's lashes came down and she melted against him.

"About those children," Sam whispered huskily after long moments had passed. "When would you like to start?"

"Now would be nice," Annie murmured.

"My thinking exactly."

Callie watched them through the French doors as their mouths met. She had witnessed this sort of behavior before and knew it would go on for some time. With a long-suffering sigh, she flopped to her stomach on the deck, front and back legs extended. With her head resting on her front paws and long ears fanned out on either side, Callie settled down to wait.

*   *   *   *   *

"GIVE YOUR HEART TO SILHOUETTE" SWEEPSTAKES
OFFICIAL RULES

NO PURCHASE NECESSARY TO ENTER OR RECEIVE A PRIZE

1. To enter and join the Silhouette Reader Service, rub off the concealment device on all game tickets. This will reveal the potential value for each Sweepstakes entry number and the number of free book(s) you will receive. Accepting the free book(s) will automatically entitle you to also receive a free bonus gift. If you do not wish to take advantage of our introduction to the Silhouette Reader Service but wish to enter the Sweepstakes only, rub off the concealment device on tickets #1-3 only. To enter, return your entire sheet of tickets. Incomplete and/or inaccurate entries are not eligible for that section or section (s) of prizes. Not responsible for mutilated or unreadable entries or inadvertent printing errors. Mechanically reproduced entries are null and void.

2. Either way, your Sweepstakes numbers will be compared against the list of winning numbers generated at random by computer. In the event that all prizes are not claimed, random drawings will be made from all entries received from all presentations to award all unclaimed prizes. All cash prizes are payable in U.S. funds. This is in addition to any free, surprise or mystery gifts that might be offered. The following prizes are awarded in this sweepstakes:

(1)	*Grand Prize	$1,000,000	Annuity
(1)	First Prize	$35,000	
(1)	Second Prize	$10,000	
(3)	Third Prize	$5,000	
(10)	Fourth Prize	$1,000	
(25)	Fifth Prize	$500	
(5000)	Sixth Prize	$5	

   *The Grand Prize is payable through a $1,000,000 annuity. Winner may elect to receive $25,000 a year for 40 years, totaling up to $1,000,000 without interest, or $350,000 in one cash payment. Winners selected will receive the prizes offered in the Sweepstakes promotion they receive.
   Entrants may cancel the Reader Service privileges at any time without cost or obligation to buy (see details in center insert card).

3. Versions of this Sweepstakes with different graphics may be offered in other mailings or at retail outlets by Torstar Corp. and its affiliates. This promotion is being conducted under the supervision of Marden-Kane, Inc., an independent judging organization. By entering this Sweepstakes, each entrant accepts and agrees to be bound by these rules and the decisions of the judges, which shall be final and binding. Odds of winning are dependent upon the total number of entries received. Taxes, if any, are the sole responsibility of the winners. Prizes are nontransferable. All entries must be received by March 31, 1990. The drawing will take place on April 30, 1990, at the offices of Marden-Kane, Inc., Lake Success, N.Y.

4. This offer is open to residents of the U.S., Great Britain and Canada, 18 years or older, except employees of Torstar Corp., its affiliates, and subsidiaries, Marden-Kane, Inc. and all other agencies and persons connected with conducting this Sweepstakes. All federal, state and local laws apply. Void wherever prohibited or restricted by law.

5. Winners will be notified by mail and may be required to execute an affidavit of eligibility and release that must be returned within 14 days after notification. Canadian winners will be required to answer a skill-testing question. Winners consent to the use of their name, photograph and/or likeness for advertising and publicity in conjunction with this and similar promotions without additional compensation. One prize per family or household.

6. For a list of our most current major prizewinners, send a stamped, self-addressed envelope to: WINNERS LIST, c/o MARDEN-KANE, INC., P.O. BOX 701, SAYREVILLE, N.J. 08871

If Sweepstakes entry form is missing, please print your name and address on a 3" x 5" piece of plain paper and send to:

In the U.S.	In Canada
Sweepstakes Entry	Sweepstakes Entry
901 Fuhrmann Blvd.	P.O. Box 609
P.O. Box 1867	Fort Erie, Ontario
Buffalo, NY 14269-1867	L2A 5X3

LTY-S69R

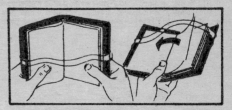

Silhouette Desire ®

COMING NEXT MONTH

#505 ODD MAN OUT—Lass Small
July's *Man of the Month*, Graham Rawlins, was undeniably attractive, but Roberta Lambert seemed uninterested. However, Graham was very determined, and she found he'd do almost *anything* to get her attention....

#506 THE PIRATE O'KEEFE—Helen R. Myers
Doctor Laura Connell was intrigued by the injured man washed up on her beach. When she discovered his true identity it was too late—she'd fallen for the pirate O'Keefe.

#507 A WILDER NAME—Laura Leone
Luke Swain was positively the most irritating man Nina Gnagnarelli had ever met. He'd insulted her wardrobe, her integrity and her manners. He'd also set her heart on fire!

#508 BLIND JUSTICE—Cathryn Clare
As far as Lily Martineau was concerned, successful corporate lawyer Matt Malone was already married—to his job. Matt pleaded guilty as charged, then demanded a retrial.

#509 ETERNALLY EVE—Ashley Summers
Nate Wright had left Eve Sheridan with a broken heart. Now he seemed to have no memory of her—but it was a night Eve would never forget!

#510 MAGIC TOUCH—Noelle Berry McCue
One magic night with a handsome stranger made Caroline Barclay feel irresistible. But she didn't believe in fairy tales until James Mitchel walked back into her life—as her new boss.

AVAILABLE NOW: